WAKING THE WILD

BETH COLLA

Edited by
TIM FERGUSON

BETH COLLA PUBLISHING

For Daisy

Author's Note

The tribe, location, and spiritual traditions in this story have been fictionalized with care. While the themes are inspired by the rich beauty of Indigenous cultures and their deep connection to nature and spirit, this story is a work of imagination.

This updated edition reflects changes made out of respect for Native communities. My hope is that this tale honors the reverence, resilience, and storytelling spirit that has long inspired me—while staying mindful of cultural integrity and respect.

1

DONUTS OF DESPAIR

I stared at the ceiling, the silence of the empty house pressing in around me. My room had a weird echo to it now that nothing was in it. I wondered if I'd feel as lost in my dreams as I did in real life.

"I hate this," I hissed between gritted teeth. Fancy Beast, my fat ragdoll cat, let out a short, judgy grumble. I was the only human she liked, as if she knew I somehow understood her best. Fancy Beast was curled up on top of me, her fluffy white mane sticking out all over the place, and she was clearly much more comfortable than I was in this crummy sleeping bag. I couldn't settle, and the sadness that this was my last night in my room was overwhelming. I despised change.

My perfect, cozy bed and all my belongings were packed for the movers in the morning. The house had just sold, and now this home, my home, this room, my room, was someone else's. We were moving to Emerald Lake, 500 miles away. I was going from 18 million people to 21,000 overnight. The culture shock was going to kill me. I had heard about Emerald Lake throughout my life, but I'd never been. My mom, Mary, and her mom, Mae, and their parents, and probably their parents, were from there, all a part of the Tuhánee tribe. My mother was half Tuhánee and her father a second-generation Italian.

My grandpa died when my mom was 19, so I never met him. My grandmother, Mae, I talked to a few times on the phone, but she and Mom had a falling out shortly after my grandfather died, so they didn't talk much. Mom left home and moved to Los Angeles and never really looked back. Sometimes I tried to find out what happened, but she wouldn't talk about it. A few months ago, Grandma Mae passed away. I came home from school and Mom was sitting on the couch staring into space; so still and quiet. She was always so active and busy; I knew something was off.

"Grandma Mae died this morning." She said matter-of-factly, her expression distant. "At some point we will need to go to Emerald and deal with the house and her things, OK?"

I remember feeling sad and confused. Mom was so warm and friendly, yet her mom had just died, and she seemed so unemotional. I chalked it up to her recent fights with my dad, and her being tired from all that drama.

I tried to imagine what Grandma Mae's house would be like. I had never even seen pictures of her. And now, as if by fate, we had a home to go to. A lake house that was ours. With the divorce, my parents had to sell our house, as Mom couldn't afford to keep it up alone. So the decision was not so much a decision as a necessity. It all happened so fast.

I felt limp, depressed, and utterly exhausted as I started to drift asleep. I was almost too tired to take the effort to fall asleep. My whole body ached from days of packing and moving things around, preparing for the worst day of my life.

Then the familiar buzzing began. I had started having these weird dreams a few months back: just as I drifted off, I would start to shake, like I was jolted by electricity, but with no pain. A loud electrical crackling sound would fill my ears. Now, as my eyes closed, I could feel the trembling and hear the buzzing. Here we go. I knew what was going to happen—I was going to pull out of my body. I just relaxed into it; I used to fight it, waking up in a panic, but that was unpleasant, so I eventually decided to try and roll with it. Plus, I didn't die after the first time, so I decided this experience must not be fatal and I was curious. The buzzing and trembling got louder and louder until *POP!* Everything went quiet. My eyes snapped open, and the familiar green sparkly filter was around everything. It was actually really beautiful, and I had this incredible ability to see 360 degrees around myself. These were not normal dreams.

It always started in the same place. I wasn't quite asleep, yet I wasn't awake, and I could see myself in my bed, as I flew around my green hazy room. I could float around the room at will, even float outside, through walls, while my body slept peacefully on the bed. Then, I was jolted into some kind of vortex, whooshing through a dark tunnel at an unbelievable speed. It wasn't frightening, because it was over very quickly, almost before I had time to be afraid. Then, I'd find myself in this grand, ancient library, shelves towering above me, filled with books containing every story ever told, or so I liked to think. I walked down the aisles, running my fingers along the spines. At the end of the shelves was a majestic fireplace with a roaring fire; I could feel the leather on my fingertips as they brushed the books, I could feel the warmth of the fire, and smell the pleasant aroma of the burning wood. All of my senses were heightened here.

The dimly lit room had high ceilings, a library ladder, and two massive sculptures of mountain lions flanked the fireplace. My heart began to beat faster as I realized I was not alone. A figure stepped out from the shadows, the tall man, dressed in a tuxedo for some inexplicable reason, with a face as familiar as my own. He looked like a movie star from the 1940's with black greased hair, tan skin, and ridiculously good looks. He smiled at me. I had seen him several times before over the last few months. Was he part of me somehow, a dream figure or a guide of sorts, maybe? I did like that he was elegant.

We would normally stand there, his odd smile feeling significant without my having any idea what it might mean, until I would find myself sucked back into the vortex, and awakening in my bed with a jolt.

But this time, he gestured to a book on a nearby table. As I stepped closer, I saw, embossed in gold on the cover, my name in all capitals and a title: *The Awakening*. That sounded dramatic. With a trembling hand, I opened the book, and as I began to read, the words came to life, playing out like a movie in my mind. A dream within a dream. The guide—I called him Frederick, for some reason —never spoke out loud to me, but I could hear his voice inside my head, reading the words from the book.

"You have a journey ahead of you. The books will guide you to your true home and purpose." His voice was gentle and soothing. I saw images coming so fast in my mind, but it was hard to decipher what they were. I saw a forest, an animal running, fog, glowing eyes, water exploding and *BOOM!*

Just as always, I was out of the dream in a flash. I bolted up awake, sweaty and feeling like I had been instantly transported back to my reality. It was intense. These dreams meant something, but I had no idea how to control them. They had started shortly after my grandma died. The first time it happened, I was so scared I thought I was losing my mind, and I wanted to tell my best friend, Robin, but I really had no idea what to say. So I just kept it to myself.

I scooted down in my sleeping bag, looking at the moon outside my window. A waxing crescent.

"Fancy Beast, is everyone as weird as I am?" I sighed picking up my phone as the time read 11:11pm. Make a wish, Robin would say.

A text from her dinged:

And with that I fell deep asleep.

The sunlight brightened my room, and the obnoxious leaf blower outside droned relentlessly on until my angry eyes opened. I sighed deeply. If sighing was an Olympic event, I would be the Simone Biles.

"Anya, wake up!" Mom yelled up to me from downstairs, "The movers are going to be here in twenty minutes! I got donuts!" Her voice was just too loud. Too loud.

"Wonderful." I sarcastically muttered.

Fancy Beast, an enthusiastic eater, stretched her girthy physique hard, splaying her toes in ways I wish I could stretch. She lumbered over to a small bowl of kibble by the cat carrier and munched away, meowing in a singsong way as she ate.

"I wish we could trade places." Fancy Beast kept chowing. I wrestled myself free from the sleeping bag and picked her up with her bowl of food, placing them both in her cat carrier. This proved to be much more of an athletic event than I had anticipated. But it would have been classic Fancy Beast to go missing on the day we were moving, so better safe than sorry.

"Sorry Lady Cakes, I'll get you some donut crumbs, OK?" Fancy Beast looked at me and whined, offended.

I had slept in my clothes, so getting dressed was not on my to-do list today. I snagged my backpack filled with my most needed items. I always needed my charging cables, headphones, candy, and grape lip balm. I grabbed some deodorant, put it on, spritzed myself with some cotton-candy perfume, and tackled my hair with my brush. The mirror inside my closet had been my favorite feature of my room as a child. I would sit and make faces at myself for hours, laughing and playacting. More recently it had become a harsh critic, picking apart my face, body and hair on a regular basis. Mom, being Tuhánee, passed down many of her features, which in theory, and to a normal person, would be a good thing. I have long straight black hair, which of course I hate. I have her high cheekbones and my skin is light, but I tan dark in the summer months, which annoys me. My eyes are my dad's, an icy blue, like a husky. I actually like my eyes, the one thing I have decided to be OK with, currently. Everyone tells me I am an exotic beauty, but most 15-year-olds are just reeling from their bodies changing into adulthood. So all we can see are the weird flaws, pimples and awkwardness. I realize this, and yet it doesn't seem to make it any better. Sigh.

The walk down the stairs to the kitchen seemed like a slow-motion montage. I saw myself at so many ages, racing up and down these stairs, happy, angry, playful, crying, with friends or alone, being carried to sleep by Mom. My entire life had been spent in this home, and now we were leaving it all behind. I felt sick. I wanted to erase everything bad.

The kitchen was filled with so many boxes and plastic-wrapped furniture, I could barely get to the island. Kettle Glazed Donuts looked back at me from a square white box. Mom knew they were my favorite. Guilt purchase. Good. I shoved a S'Mores donut in my mouth and took a huge sip of coffee. Oh God, the perfect combination. Why do donuts and coffee taste so exquisite together? I started drinking coffee last year, when I was 14, to my parents' horror. For some reason, when your teen begins to drink coffee it's all over. Childhood is completely gone, or at least that's what my dad said. Although now he was completely gone, with his new 27-year-old girlfriend and her two kids. I cringe just thinking about the chaos over the last year. His midlife crisis ruining everything, taking everyone down.

"Honey, did you put Fancy Beast in the cat carrier?" Mom power-walked into the kitchen like she was trying to win some race. Her black hair was on top of her head in a messy bun, and she was dressed in sweats with no makeup. She really looked like garbage, and for the thousandth time this year I felt bad for her.

"Yes." I said. My sentences these days were getting shorter and shorter.

"Thank you Anya." Mom kissed my head and hugged me, smiling. "I know today is a lot. But soon we'll be on the road and hey, let's try and make the road trip fun."

"OK." Mouth full of donut.

Robin came running into the house, breathless.

"Hey I overslept! I was scared I missed you!" Robin was a tiny blonde with big brown eyes and a really loud, raspy voice. She's the loudest person I know, and it's one of my favorite things about her. It's unexpected.

"Still here." I smirked, doing a little jig.

"Ooh, Kettle Glazed." Robin widened her eyes as she coyly helped herself to a maple bar with a two finger pinch, "Don't mind if I do."

"Best donuts in town." I laughed as I jammed another donut of despair directly into my mouth hole.

"So what's the ETA? When do we hide me in the trunk?" Robin said, sparkling with mischief.

"I heard that!" Mom bellowed from the back of the house.

"Of course you did, it's ROBIN." I screamed her name in my best Robin impression. We laughed, almost crying. We had cried so much over the last month, dreading this day, the separation, the move, the huge changes. The ironic thing was I didn't like loud noises, but for some reason Robin's loudness delighted me.

The first time I saw her, she was walked into our second-grade classroom by our principal, Mr. Brosnan.

"Class, this is our new student, Robin Shines. She just moved to Los Angeles from Texas. Everyone say hello to Robin and make her feel welcome." Principal Brosnan smiled as he turned to leave the classroom back to our teacher, Mrs. Dunn.

A dreary hello came in unison from thirty-five tired second graders. To everyone's shock Robin piped up with her bigger-than-life voice. The principal even stopped in his tracks and turned around.

"Hi class, I'm Robin! Did you know the state bird in Texas is the northern mockingbird!? I guess your bird is the quail. My dad used to hunt quail in Texas, so I've eaten a lot of quails, but not mockingbirds."

The class looked at Robin with mouths agape.

I immediately wanted to be her best friend. And in a strange Universal convergence, that actually happened.

***

The movers were swiftly carrying everything out of our house and into their giant truck. They moved fast, and before long everything in the kitchen was on the truck.

I wanted more time. I had drawn a skull and crossbones on April 3rd and checked off the days leading up to the dreaded move; and now it was here. I needed more time. Transitions and I don't do well together. I was told it's a neurodivergent trait. How was I going to survive this without Robin? As if she knew what I was thinking, she grabbed my hands.

"Listen, we live in the modern age. We can FaceTime. We can Zoom. We can Google Meet, we can Marco Polo, we can call, we can write letters. We can send smoke signals. We can do this." Robin was shaking her head in affirmation.

"We can do this." I repeated.

"It's only 8 hours and 11 minutes by car. 90 minutes to Reno by airplane." Robin looked optimistic.

"And 11 minutes?" I said, excessively blinking, eyebrows raised.

"Yes, I checked." Robin chimed. "Repeatedly."

Mom came down the stairs carrying Fancy Beast. She set her down next to me. Robin peeked into the carrier and the Beast hissed and snarled.

"That cat hates me. Even on this day of goodbye, she can't even muster a courtesy meow." Robin scrunched her face at Fancy Beast and hissed back.

"She only likes me." I said proudly.

"Well, you are part feline." Robin joked.

"I wish I was full feline. I would sleep the entire car ride to Emerald Lake and hold my urine."

"Eww!" Robin winced.

Mom breezed in the room again, like her feet were on fire.

"The movers are pretty much done. I'm going to do a last minute idiot check." Mom wasn't really talking to us, but more like announcing herself to anyone who cared.

"Well, this is it." Robin let out a deep breath and picked up my backpack as I schlepped Fancy Beast.

We walked to the car in silence. The movers were standing by to latch the truck shut upon Mom's approval. Our Subaru was packed pretty tight with the things we wanted accessible. There was a space right behind the driver's seat where Fancy Beast's carrier would go. Our bikes were secured to the back rack, and a cooler filled with snacks and drinks was comfortably in arm's reach.

Mom came rushing out of the house, locking the door behind her, and putting the keys in the lockbox that our Realtor left on the spigot. She waved an OK to the movers, who again went into rush mode and locked the truck up tight.

"Thank you! See you in Emerald!" Mom waved to the movers cheerfully, who smiled and waved back. *Why is she so cheerful,* I thought, annoyed.

I stood next to the passenger door looking at Robin, whose eyes were welled with tears.

We hugged so hard I thought we'd kill each other, our ribs shattered to smithereens.

"Text me from the road. Send me pictures of weird things. You know how much I like weird things. And remember summer vacation starts in 71 days." Robin laughed, wiping away fat tears.

"71 days," I said, getting into the car and putting down the window. Our hands were ripped apart by the car pulling out of the driveway.

As the car drove away I looked back. Robin was standing in front of our house, which was no longer our house, waving frantically.

The ball in my throat was expanding. I reclined the seat back so I was looking at the headliner. The hot tears rolled back over my cheekbones and filled my ears. They crackled. I had become an expert at silent crying. Mom had her eyes on the road, the podcast she liked droning on; I could have a full meltdown in absolute silence. I'm not sure that was healthy, but it was a skill I acquired this year as I strained to hear my parent's hushed arguments, my fears becoming more real with each fight they had. I cried through these arguments alone, but also in unison with my mother, as she wept in the other room. I didn't want her to know I heard everything. Things I wished I didn't know.

My father was in love with someone else. She was "amazing" and needed him. He didn't mean for it to happen, of course. The gross narcissism soaked into our hearts as we both realized my father was just not a very good person. He had always been off or distant, but I remember loving him so much as a child. I wanted his approval and affection, neither of which I felt I ever got. Mom made up for it in spades though. Her love was pure, and I always knew she was there for me. She took care of me when I was sick, when I had bad dreams, and when I felt sad. Lately I had so much guilt. I knew she needed more from me, but I was so wound up in my own pain that I wasn't a very good daughter. I was distant and cool. Maybe this move would bring us closer together. I wanted it to.

The car ride was a blur of tears and silence. I watched the familiar streets of LA pass by in a haze, feeling numb as we left the city and headed towards the unknown. As we drove further away from everything I had ever known, the reality of the situation began to sink in. I was leaving my home, my friends, and my old life behind. I felt a sense of loss and grief wash over me as I realized that things would never be the same again. The trajectory of my life had just taken a radical shift.

We stopped for gas and snacks a few hours outside of Emerald Lake. I got out of the car, stretching my legs and feeling the crisp mountain air on my face. I looked up at the towering trees and big sky, feeling small and insignificant in the vast wilderness. I took a deep breath, filling my lungs with the fresh scent of pine and earth. It was quiet, peaceful, and a world away from the hustle and smog of Los Angeles. I felt a twinge of excitement amidst the sadness. Maybe this move would be a chance for a new beginning, or maybe I was hallucinating from breathing real, fresh air for once.

I walked towards the mini-mart and saw an old payphone off to the side that looked to be in working order. I snapped a shot of it for Robin. There was also a jerky stand set up with some super skinny guy in a top hat wearing a rabbit suit, selling various types of jerky and rugs. Nothing like a good rug to eat your jerky on, I chuckled to myself. *Snap!* Pics of weird stuff for Robin completed.

Back in the car, I settled into the passenger seat with a bag of Ruffles and a Dr. Pepper. Fancy Beast meowed softly from her carrier, and I reached in to give her a scratch behind the ears and shared a chip. She purred loudly, her rumbling purrs vibrating through the car as she crunched down on the potato chip. She had always amazed everyone with her appetite for weird human foods. Ruffles. Pickles. And most amazing of all, grapefruit. I smiled, feeling a sense of comfort and companionship from my little fat pal. As we continued our journey, I gazed out at the passing scenery. I kept seeing signs that read NO FRACKING and KEEP Emerald BLUE.

Mom had been silent most of the drive, lost in her own thoughts, I guess. She turned off the podcast she was half listening to, and I could feel her wanting to talk to me.

"Anya." She probed to see if I was awake.

"I'm awake." I replied with my eyes closed.

"Robin can come visit anytime. She can stay as long as she wants. You know, Emerald in the summer is really fun. The lake and the weather is beautiful. Lots of hiking and boating." Mom was trying to cheer me up and I loved her for it, but I just couldn't whip up any enthusiasm.

"OK." I opened my eyes and gazed at the trees. There were no palm trees here. Just needle trees. Needles pointed at me from every direction.

"Do we have a boat?" I asked curiously.

"Yes, I think we probably still do. We had canoes and a speedboat in the boathouse."

"Yeah, but wasn't that like a hundred years ago." I mocked.

"Take it easy. I'm not *that* old." Mom mused.

As we approached our new home, I admired the sunset, displaying a beautiful array of oranges and pinks. It was dazzling. Mom slowed down as she drove onto Pine Needle Way. She seemed to be scanning the homes along the route, gathering memories. A deer jumped out on the road and Mom swerved the car.

"Golly!" She shrieked.

My heart skipped a beat and I stared at the deer, who stared right back at me. What was just seconds felt like minutes.

"Golly?!" I said back to Mom, sort of dumbfounded that was her best exclamation.

"Seriously, Anya, are you making fun of me? I get scared half to death and all you can do is criticize my, my, word choice?" Mom was annoyed.

I felt bad. She was right.

"I'm sorry. I didn't mean to be snarky." I said, genuinely remorseful. Then Mom looked at me for a minute with very serious eyes, and immediately started busting out laughing. I started laughing too.

"Well, welcome to Emerald Lake. The animals are greeting us Tuhánee women already. " Mom smiled affectionately.

We turned onto our street and pulled into the driveway of a gorgeous lake house.

The car came to a stop, and I felt a wave of dizziness as I stepped out. I was overwhelmed by the fresh scent of the lake and the surrounding forest. The air was cool, and I shivered as I took in the view. Our new home was a classic two-story log cabin, with a wide porch that overlooked the lake. I could see the moon reflecting on the water, and I felt a sense of peace wash over me. "It's breathtaking, Mom." I said, my voice soft with wonder.

"I know, honey." She smiled at me, her eyes shining with unshed tears. "Let's go inside and explore your new home. It's been in our family for a very long time. We can unpack the car tomorrow." I nodded, still taking in the view. The cabin was surrounded by tall pine trees dusted in snow, their needles reaching towards the starry sky. The air was filled with the sound of crickets and the gentle lapping of the lake against the shore. A bird flew right at me and then veered off erratically.

"God, that bird is drunk!" I exclaimed.

"Ha! That's a bat." Mom laughed.

"Bats? We have bats here!?" I forgot to be depressed for a second.

"We have bats here. We have lots of animals. You'll see." Mom dragged a small suitcase up the steps, banging on each step and onto the porch. She fished around in her purse looking for the keys.

"Mom has anyone been here since Grandma Mae passed?" I asked wondering.

"Your Auntie Lily has been keeping an eye on things and taking in the mail."

"Auntie Lily?" I was shocked. Why do I know nothing of this Auntie Lily? I set Fancy Beast down on the porch, my backpack slung over my shoulder.

"A great Auntie, yes. Grandma Mae's sister. She is my mother's younger sister; she's seventy-four, I think." Mom informed me.

I stood on the porch, out of breath, waiting for Mom to open the door. A flutter of moths were fighting for the porch light.

"Why am I so out of breath? That was like seven stair steps." I looked down the steps from the porch, disgusted with myself.

"Because we're now at over 6,000 feet above sea level. The air is thinner up here, and you aren't used to that. So give it a week, and you'll acclimate just fine. Until then, you may be tired, dizzy, and out of breath." Mom had opened the front door, and she reached in to switch on the lights. This was nothing like our Spanish-style home in Los Feliz. The warm glow of the light cast a shadow into the large open living area: tall ceilings, made from logs, big windows overlooking a shimmering lake, and a massive fireplace made of river rocks. I stepped inside adjusting my eyes to the dim light. It smelled like old people.

"Sorry, let me get more lights on in here." Mom fumbled with her suitcase as she walked into the living room and switched on the giant wagon-wheel chandelier, which hung from the top of the pitched ceiling, over the living area. It was magnificent. Along the sides of the fireplace were woven baskets filled with fire wood and newspaper. I noticed these baskets with beautiful patterns all over the living room- some small, some large. There were paintings and sculptures throughout the home. This was a beautifully kept cabin, and I felt an instant connection to it even though it was like nothing I had ever seen.

"Wow." I couldn't think of more words to say.

"Yeah, I know." Mom shook her head and pointed up the stairs. "Go pick a room, sweetheart. You have five to choose from, so whatever feels like you. The one to the left of the stairs is mine." Mom smiled weakly, weary from the drive and just... everything. "I'm going to take a bath and go to bed. I'm out of gas."

Before I explored upstairs I let Fancy Beast out of her carrier and set up her litter box in a corner of the laundry room, where I also put her food and water. She scratched around the box, but mostly did her low-to-the-ground ninja walk through the cabin, exploring and sniffing every inch.

"No territorial pissing, Beast." I sternly reminded. Fancy Beast jogged inches from the floor and under the large leather couch, a perfect den.

I could hear the pipes strain from lack of use as Mom's bath filled up. The heater kicked on, and the house had that weird burnt-metal smell that happens when the heater hasn't been turned on forever. I grabbed a blanket from the couch and wrapped it around me. It was freezing, and it was going to take a while for this huge cabin to heat up. I ran my hands along the thick, wooden bannisters, obviously hand-carved a long time ago. The wood was so smooth and worn, beautifully so. The stairs creaked, and I looked up at the pitched ceiling. Fancy Beast had left her den and was coming up the stairs behind me, sticking close. I could hear the water faucets squeaking shut as Mom turned off the bathwater. A large open walkway, looking down over the living area, spanned the length of the cabin. The doors to the bedrooms were shut. I went slowly down the walkway, looking at the art that was hanging all up and down the tall living room walls. Oil paintings of the Lake were everywhere. Running my hands along the smooth wood of the railings was pleasant and calming.

Then, almost as if it were audible to anyone present, I heard the words "You have a journey ahead of you. The books will guide you to your true home."

I froze in place and scanned the room. "Frederick?" I whispered. But I heard nothing except the purring of Fancy Beast doing figure eights around my legs.

One of the doors at the end of the walkway seemed to have a light green glow coming out from beneath the door. I headed to it and reached for the brass doorknob, slowly opening it. The glow was gone once I was inside. I walked over to the built-in bookshelves, filled with books, and selected an old book that was sticking out from the rest. The title read, "Pathways." As soon as I picked it up I swear I saw the title letters glow. Standing there staring at the book, I waited for something to happen. Just then my phone dinged and it was Robin. The text notification startled me so much I dropped the book and sat back onto the bed, laughing at my nerves.

Are you there yet?

I sent Robin the pictures I took earlier and hit send.

Robin hearted the pictures as I fell back onto the bed, worn out. But I found my room. This was my room. A large but cozy space with a wall of books, there was an old tanker desk in the corner which had an ancient black typewriter on it and a small desk lamp. The large bed was super soft with huge pillows, and a ridiculously adorable needlepoint quilt showing scenes of raccoons sledding and deer drinking from a creek. The wooden headboard had beautifully carved pinecone motifs, which matched a highboy dresser and the two nightstands. Each night stand had a set of hobnailed lamps with green milk-glass shades. An oversized leather chair with a wool blanket draped over it was next to the window, looking out at the lake. A bathroom was attached to the bedroom; it had a clawfoot tub and little octagon tiled flooring.

There was a door that went out to a deck that overlooked the lake. A small couch was on the deck and a little side table. A staircase led down to the beach front. It looked as though we had our own pier that jutted out over the lake, and at the end a little boathouse. I stepped out into the cold air and looked out on the lake. It was incredible, stretching out past the horizon like an ocean, shimmering under the very last light of sunset. The snow on the pines seemed to glow from within, just from its dazzling, ever-present whiteness. In spite of everything, I felt suddenly peaceful.

Heading back into the room, I noticed more of those distinct baskets; they were all around. A large painting hung above the bed of the lake at sunset with the words Oma'shélun painted in the sky, as clouds. Which should have made it weird and cheesy, but it was beautiful. I strained to see the signature at the bottom, and made out Mae Carlucci. My grandmother painted this! I touched the painting with my hand and felt my palm tingle.

"I see you found your room." Mom stood in the doorway in a robe, with her hair wrapped up in a towel.

"Jeez, you scared the crap out of me." I whipped around to confront her.

"I'm so sorry honey, I didn't mean to startle you." Mom eyed the book on the bed. "Where did you get that book?" she asked.

I gestured to the WALL of books with a flair of *obviously*.

Mom furrowed her brow, and looked at me for a moment longer than made sense.

"What?" I said, defensive.

"Nothing." Mom blew me a kiss. "Let's get some sleep. The movers will be by early in the morning. It should warm up soon in here, but if you're too cold I suggest taking a hot bath. It did me good."

I nodded and patted the bed for Fancy Beast to jump up. Mom shuffled down the walkway in her fuzzy slippers. The sound of her walking around in her slippers was always comforting to me. It was the noise of early mornings while she made coffee, and quietly tidied the house while I slept in. The hushed busyness of her feet getting things done while I lingered in that sleepy delirium—it was home. It was her.

I picked up the book and looked at the cover. It was leather, obviously quite old, and in gold ornate writing it read Pathways. I opened the book and inside was writing:

Mae James

Lily James

F. James -1930

A black-and-white photograph fell out. It was of a woman at an easel, painting. She had her back to the camera; her canvas was visible and in the background, the lake. *Mae, 1961.* I stared at the photo, wondering who took the picture of my young Grandmother Mae.

I turned the pages of the book and no words were there, just blank pages. It smelled old and musty, but I loved it. I always liked the smell of old books and I put my nose right in the spine where the two pages met, breathing in the years.

"Weird," I whispered, as I put the totally blank book on the night stand. I twisted the switch on the milk-glass lamp off, and the only light that shone in was from the hint of the moon. My eyes felt heavy, and Fancy Beast pressed against me in a cozy sleep. Her rhythmic breathing lulled me as I joined her in deep slumber.

The next morning Mom was up early, buzzing around preparing for the movers. I dreaded the commotion and chaos. Mom knew this, and suggested I venture into town and explore. She gave me some spending money, and told me to Uber there while she was dealing with the movers. I think she just wanted me out of her hair, which was fine by me.

I ordered the Uber and was shocked they even had Ubers up here. I drank the rest of my coffee and finished off my eggs. I put the plate on the floor for Fancy Beast to lick clean. She scooted the plate across the floor as she licked, her name tag clanging against the plate rhythmically.

"Mom, make sure Fancy Beast doesn't escape while the movers are here!" I yelled, as I was about to walk out the door to meet the car.

"I'll put her in the carrier Anya. Have fun! Text me while you're out so I know you're still alive." Mom yelled back.

"Morbid, Mom. Morbid." I left the house, probably not dressed warmly enough for the weather.

A small white Toyota was waiting in the driveway, the driver was a female. Only 10% of serial killers were women, so I felt good about my odds. I had a knack for knowing random statistics. I climbed in the car. It was warm and smelled like piña coladas. The backseat had a small basket of Starbursts. The Uber lady was a pro.

"The directions just said Bearbrook. Where are you going specifically?" The driver looked back at me in the rear view mirror; her knit hat had a big pink pompom on top.

"I don't know. I need to be out of the house to avoid the movers. I guess I'm trying to kill some time. Any good shopping areas?" I asked, blowing heat into my hands, which have been permanently cold since arriving in Emerald.

"Well, I like Prince Beach. They have some good vintage stores. But that's about a 30 minute drive." The Uber driver was adjusting her maps.

"Let's take a drive." I suggested.

We headed down West Lakewood Boulevard. I looked out the window at the snow on the roofs sliding off and counted a lot of ski racks. I saw signs for a state park, and up ahead a guy was putting a sandwich board out in front of a deli.

Up ahead I saw a sign that read: *Dan Gann The Souvenir Man!! 1 mile.*

"Excuse me, can we make a stop at the souvenir shop?" Robin is a connoisseur of kitsch, and I could tell this place would be brimming with awful knick-knacks. "OK." She turned into the lot.

The souvenir shack was an old log cabin, modest to begin with and poorly kept up. A painted, faded sign above the door had a cartoon of someone who had to be Dan Gann; he was sporting a loud plaid blazer like some kind of 1970s TV host, which seemed at odds with the general Sasquatch vibe of the shop. There were several chainsaw-carved bears and totems out front, chained to an ill-shaped lump of concrete slab. The Uber lady parked and kept the engine running.

"Do you want me to wait? I imagine you won't be long." She said, amused. Little did she know the crappiness was what I was there for. "Sure. I think I'll find what I'm looking for."

I got out of the car and walked up to the front door, pushing it in to open it. A cacophony of terrible-sounding bells all jangled, announcing my arrival. Apparently, my arrival was unnoticed because a man was yelling at the employee behind the counter and he didn't stop on my account.

"Listen, when I tell you to deliver a package, I expect you to do it right away." The man yelled, pointing a fat finger in the employee's face. "These are not people who like to wait!"

The employee, a young guy probably in his late teens, looked at the man with slack disdain, moving his head back like a turtle retreating into his shell. "I delivered it this morning. They got it. OK? I was feeling sick last night."

"Because all you eat is candy!" The man turned around quickly to make a dramatic exit, when he saw me standing in the doorway, staring. He had aged, but the cartoon didn't lie: It was Dan Gann himself. The Souvenir Man, no less. He was a smallish, stocky man, looking like a high-school football player past his prime. His fingers were like tight little sausages on a hot grill, trying to bust out of their casings. His hair was thick and sandy, combed down so rigidly it almost seemed like a wig. His sport coat and slacks looked as though they had fit at one time, but now they strained at the seams.

"Oh, please come in. I didn't see you there," he said, his voice now sounding like an actor in a black-and-white film. "Please do let Russell know if there is anything you need." Dan snapped his fingers at Russell, who in turn exhibited quality stink eye.

"Thank you?" I said as a question.

Dan Gann stormed out of the building, bells jingling. I looked at

Russell; Russell looked at me. He sighed. "A-hole," he finally blurted out, while he opened a fresh bag of Nerd Clusters.

I wandered around the store, awkwardly. A display of shot glasses lined a dusty shelf. Yellowed posters of the lake lined the knotty-pine walls. There were t-shirts and a shelf full of expired sunscreen. I looked around for the advertised "Indian artifacts" but was having trouble seeing anything.

"Excuse me Russell?" I quietly said. Russell looked startled that I knew his name. "Where are the Indian artifacts?"

"Well, we're out of the baskets, but those are coming in soon, I guess. They're fake and I don't care who knows it. I do have some beaded belts over by the sunscreen. Actual Indians might have made those, I'm not sure. I might have an arrowhead here in the take-a-penny jar." Russell poked a sticky finger in the jar, making an effort to look.

I pondered why there would be an arrowhead in the jar for a moment, and gave up. "It's OK. I'm good. I'll just browse around a minute." I backed away from Russell slowly and headed towards the sunscreen. Underneath the shelf, way back on a hook, was one beaded belt that looked to be sized for a baby's waist. I picked it up and tried to picture a small infant needing a belt.

I scanned the room, and a box piled full of stuffed animals caught my attention. There was a bear puppet, some mice in skirts, and under-neath, something that looked like some kind of bird. I pulled it out from the bottom of the box. It was black and had wings like an eagle, but had scales on the body like a fish. The face was all messed up too, like an angry baby was sewn onto a fish- bird body. My God, this was incredible! I had to get it for Robin. There was no price tag on it, but it was magnificent. No price was too high for this gem.

I walked back up to Russell and deposited the stuffed whatever the heck it was onto the counter for purchase. I also picked up a pack of off-brand gum in an appealingly retro wrapper that was in a box next to the penny jar.

"You don't want to put that in your mouth," was all Russell said. I looked at him suspiciously, and slowly put the gum back.

Russell looked at the stuffy and narrowed his eyes, thinking.

"Just give me five bucks." Russell said.

I was reaching into my pocket to get the cash when Russell added. "You know what, it's on the house. Take it. Dan is such a turd, I hope he goes bankrupt. Although that's unlikely because he sells illegal artifacts from the back room. But hey, you didn't hear that from me, his employee of the month." Russell rolled his eyes hard. He was over it. Back behind the counter, on a corkboard, was a printout of Russell smiling big, doing the double thumbs up, tacked to the board. In Sharpie underneath it said: Employee of the Month.

"Thank you and, oh, congratulations." I took the stuffed toy off the counter, putting it in my bag I started to walk out the door.

"Thank you." Russell sneezed.

I walked out to the car. The Uber lady was on the phone having an animated conversation with someone.

I tapped on the window and she unlocked the door, hanging up the phone.

"So was it everything you hoped it would be?" She asked.

"Better." I said.

2

———

P-22

The Emerald wind whipped around me, biting at my cheeks and sending shivers down my spine. After a week of living here, I was nowhere near used to the weather. I pulled my jacket tighter around my slight frame, my breath fogging in the crisp air, as I trudged towards the imposing brick building that was Emerald High. Still shaking from the cold, I pulled a knit cap out of my jacket pocket and pulled it over my unruly hair. I looked up at the huge, old doors, leading into school. It felt more like a fortress than a school, its stone walls seemingly designed to keep out the world, not welcome it in. Two giant carved wooden bears stood on each side of the entrance. One wore a red scarf that someone had obviously crocheted. The other held a tiny pennant that said Go Bears. I felt like I was on another planet.

It wasn't that long ago I had been watching the classic horror flick *Carrie,* with Robin and our friends at the Hollywood Cemetery. They showed movies there on the side of the mausoleum. It was so cool; sitting on the lawn, soaking in the buzz of everyone picnicking and dancing to the DJ. It was one of my favorite things to do on hot LA evenings. I loved being surrounded by the busy energy of traffic and helicopters. Hollywood was just different than anyplace else, and I missed it. I missed the pink sunsets of magic hour. I missed the energy and how everyone had valet parking. I missed ridiculously expensive smoothies with pretentious ingredients. Now, I was a stranger in a world of towering pines and silent, snow-dusted streets. You had to park your own car here. There were no smoothies that I could find. My parents' divorce had thrown my life into a whirlwind, and here I was, forced to trade my happy, social, old life for the hushed, almost eerie quiet of Emerald Lake. I felt completely alone.

I clutched my backpack, its weight a physical manifestation of the burden I was carrying. The weight of change, of uncertainty, of a life upended.

The school doors groaned open as I pushed against them, the familiar metallic scent of lockers and industrial cleansers flooding my senses. Well, at least that was the same. A wave of nervous energy pulsed through the hallways, a symphony of chattering voices and clanging doors opening and slamming shut. I'm just an outsider, my wet Vans and faded Griffith Park t-shirt standing out in a sea of North Face jackets and Sorel snow boots.

I navigated the maze of hallways, the floor plan a foreign language I couldn't decipher yet. Eventually, I found my locker, a cold, steel box adorned with a faded sticker of a mountain lion. There it was again, the lion. I thought of P-22, the famous Hollywood mountain lion that lived in Griffith Park. P-22 had become sick, and with his malnourishment began attacking neighborhood pets. Sadly, he was put down. I cried so hard that day. I missed knowing he was roaming the hills, a wild animal surrounded by a completely urban setting. There was something so wondrous about that, and I had felt such a strong connection to him. I smiled wistfully, lost in thought, when I was startled by a voice.

"You lost?"

I looked up, surprised anyone was speaking to me. Standing before me was a really... hot guy with a mop of dark, wild hair, his eyes a light blue, similar to my own. He wore a black leather jacket, his jeans scuffed at the knees, a touch of rebellion in his stance that made him seem a world apart from the sporty ski crowd that surrounded us. *Be cool, Anya*, I thought to myself, *be cool*.

"I'm Ethan Sloan," he said, extending a hand. "You're new here, right?"

I smiled, unguarded, a warmth spreading through my chest at his easygoing charm. "Yeah, Anya. Anya Petrova. I just moved here from LA." I returned the formal handshake.

"Ohh LA. Fancy. Welcome to Emerald Lake," Ethan said, his smile widening. "It might feel a little different at first, but you'll get used to it. It's a good place to be, trust me. And way less traffic. So Anya, is that Russian?"

I laughed nervously. "My dad is half Russian, half jerk. My mom is Tuhánee and Italian."

"Whoa. There's a lot there to unpack. Half jerk. A story behind that for sure." I felt a curious pull toward him. I mean sure, he looked gorgeous, but there was something more to him, a confidence and an energy that was alluring.

"Oh there's a story." The bell rang. I winced. Too loud. Too loud. Ethan noticed my discomfort and put his hands over my ears.

"Those bells are vile." He gestured towards the hallway. "Follow me," he said. "I'll show you around. What's your first class?"

I unfolded a wrinkled piece of paper from my pocket.

"Media Tech," I said.

"Media Tech. OK. Mr. Mathews. He's cool. I know the way." Ethan grabbed my hand, as we weaved our way through the crowded hallways, watching everyone scurry to class. *My God, he was holding my hand—was it sweaty?*

He introduced me to a few of his friends, in passing, with rushed hellos. All of them seemingly as comfortable and familiar with each other as Ethan was with the school itself.

As I found my place in Media Tech class, I couldn't shake the feeling that something about this place, about Ethan, was different. I mean, definitely different than Hollywood. He waved goodbye as he left me in class and went to his own homeroom. I sat in front of my computer just staring at the screen, overwhelmed.

I managed to find all of my classes and the day flew by, filled with a bewildering amount of introductions and confusing schedules; names I would forget and faces I would struggle to remember. I spent lunch in the library, needing the quiet. I put my headphones on, the ones that could cancel sounds out. I sighed a silent relief. I was fumbling to find my footing in this new environment, my city-born sensibilities clashing cultures with the rugged, almost mystical aura of Emerald. There was a stillness and a pace I would have to get used to here.

Sitting in my last class and waiting for the school bell to ring, I sighed, wishing I could simply disappear back into the comfort of my old life with my old friends. I longed for two parents, warm weather and excellent Mexican food. As I gathered my books, I felt a tap on my shoulder.

I turned to find a girl with a mass of curly red hair and a smattering of freckles across her nose. She wore a pair of oversized black glasses that magnified her bright green eyes, giving her a curious, wide-eyed look.

"Hey," she said, her voice soft and friendly. "I'm Iris. I saw you with Ethan earlier. You're new, right?" I nodded, a sense of wariness creeping over me. *OMG she's going to bully me. She's going to beat me up and tell me to stay the hell away from Ethan.* I braced myself, curling my fists.

"Well, I just wanted to say hi and that if you ever need anything, feel free to come find me. When it's still cold we sit in the cafeteria by the vending machines during lunch. Come find us. We can give you all the gossip on Emerald High. Ethan can be a bit... vague about the important stuff." Iris winked, her expression conspiratorial.

What was happening? I un-balled my fist and without processing the idea that Iris might just be a nice person, I spewed out, "Thanks," I managed a small, awkward smile. "I'm Anya."

"I know," Iris said with a grin, not quite looking at me. "Ethan mentioned you. See you at lunch tomorrow, Anya."

I wasn't used to making friends so easily, and the attention was a little much. Did that just happen? I was invited to lunch?

I watched Iris walk away, my curiosity piqued. I noticed she was wearing an animal tail attached to her back belt loop. Wow, the trends in Emerald were way different than Los Angeles. I felt a strange sense of intrigue as I thought about Ethan and his group of friends. I mean, who is that friendly so fast? I felt on guard, yet I also felt ridiculous for being so paranoid. I could never really read people.

I took the bus home and walked up the porch stairs to the cabin, still out of breath. The door was unlocked, and I walked in to find a fire going. The cabin was warm and inviting. It smelled like apple cider, burning wood and cookies. Mom had been tidying the place, still unpacking some of our things. She also baked some of her famous oatmeal-butterscotch cookies. It was slowly becoming home.

"Hey, how was your first day?" Mom had a cookie in her hand and stuffed it in my mouth as she helped me take off my backpack.

"Mmm prhemjfnknfosfn grmmmd" I said with the cookie jammed in my mouth.

"I see." Mom laughed. Chewed and swallowed, tried again.

"Umm, it was pretty good... the people are shockingly nice here." I said, finishing off the cookie.

"Yeah that's a big problem with Emerald Lake. All the kindness." Mom was in a good mood. I felt relieved to see some of her tension gone and her humor back. The move was behind us, the divorce almost final, and she was now able to really try to move forward.

"Did you make any friends?" she asked. I noticed she had makeup on today.

"Maybe. One boy was really helpful. Ethan, Ethan Sloan I think?"

"Sloan?" Mom's eyes widened.

"Yeah, and?" I asked, annoyed. I could get annoyed over the dumbest stuff these days.

"Oh nothing. I knew a Sloan family growing up here. Maybe he's related." Mom tried to act nonchalant, but I could tell there was something going on there. I was too tired to investigate further, and just wanted to go to my room and fall into a brain-rot hole on my phone with Fancy Beast by my side.

"OK, well, I'm going to my room." I started up the stairs.

"You know, that used to be Grandma Mae's painting studio. Before she made it a guest room. She spent a lot of time in there." Mom shared.

I stood mid-stairs pondering this information. I was so unfamiliar with learning anything about my mom's side of the family, I almost didn't know how to react.

"OK." I gestured a *whatever* with my hands, without even turning around, and headed to my room.

God, I'm a jerk.

In my room, I immediately laid down on the bed. I loved this room. The lake views were intoxicating and the room had a very easy feel to it. I hadn't even unpacked any of my decor items from the moving boxes yet. I was kind of enjoying the typewriter, bookshelf look that was going on. It was vintage. Real vintage. Fancy Beast came out from under the bed, where she had taken up space most of the week. She snuggled next to me, where I proceeded to pet all her favorite spots. My mind was worn out. All the newness was giving me a bad case of the sleeps. My eyes were so heavy. I couldn't keep them open.

The buzzing. The loud buzzing vibrated my whole body. The static snap, and—*whoosh*—I was popped out of my physical body. Floating like Charlie and Grandpa, filled with the fizzy lifting drink from *Willy Wonka & the Chocolate Factory*. I had no control, spastically tossed around in midair while my body rested next to Fancy Beast.

Pathways was on the nightstand, and it opened up. The pages were filled with text and photos, but I couldn't read anything. I was up too high, and the pages were flipping by too quickly. I tried to reach for the book, but was pulled back by some force, and was instantly hurtling through a dark tunnel, lights flickering past me at great speed. Boom! Within an instant I was standing in the ancient library: fireplace crackling, mountain lions in place, and the endless shelves of books. Frederick appeared next to the sculptures, and as he placed his hands on the head of the mountain lions the eyes lit up a bright blue. I was frozen in place, transfixed by the bright blue eyes. I heard Frederick's voice. "The path will be revealed, Anya. Your purpose will be clear." It was the first time he said my name, and with that, I was back in my body.

My eyes opened, adjusting to the darkness. I could hear Mom humming downstairs in the kitchen. The smell of garlic permeated the air and roused me to get up. I stood by the bed, woozy. The book was closed on the nightstand. I picked it up and flipped through it again. Sniffed it. No words, just blank pages like before, and the photograph tucked inside. Not like the dream. I set the book down and made my way to the kitchen. Food, bath and bed were the order of the night.

Mornings were hard for me. Doing everything I needed to do in time to get anywhere was usually a challenge. I always got distracted by something else and I took my time. Time was the bane of my existence. It made my dad so frustrated; he prided himself on his punctuality. I remember many times when he sat in the car, waiting for me to be ready. He just lived in exasperation, especially the last few years. He had no patience for me, and I felt like I was constantly apologizing to him for who I was. It was really sad he had just vanished from our lives. Did he care? I missed the idea of him being around, but if I was super honest with myself, I didn't miss the tension.

I set three alarms starting at 5:45 a.m. —the only way I stand a chance of making it to school on time. Usually by alarm #3 I was vertical. I figured out if I put my clothes out the night before it saved me twenty minutes. If I wore them to bed, thirty minutes. The weather was cold and a little drizzly, so I went looking in the closet for my rain boots. They barely ever got used in Los Angeles, and now I was pretty sure they were going to see some real action here. I scanned deep in the closet and saw something I hadn't noticed before. There was a little door inside the back of the closet! It was a little less than half the size of the closet door. I crouched down and moved some of the boxes I had thrown in there. The doorknob was cold and metal, with a stamped design of an owl. I twisted it and pushed the door open. Immediately it smelled like, I don't know, weird, like a combination of linseed oil and hundred-year-old dust.

It was too dark to see, so I came back into my room and got a flashlight that I had found in the nightstand the day before.

Back in the closet I aimed the light into the dark little mini closet. It was actually bigger in there than I thought, and seemed to have yet another door at the other end. Oh, it was a passageway to the other bedroom! Inside the corridor were tons of paintings. Maybe about fifty, all different sizes and in various stages of completion. I also saw boxes of art supplies and paints. Bottles of oils and rags. I grabbed one of the boxes and it had layers of thick dust on top of it. I flipped open the lid and flashed the light inside. I saw a bunch of different animal masks, beautifully carved from wood, some skillfully adorned with feathers, and others with what looked like real animal hides. The masks were all kinds of animals: owls, deer, bears, mountain lions, and skunks. There were also raccoon tails and what looked like real fox tails.

"Anya!! You're going to miss the bus!" Mom yelled from downstairs. My mother's life was an endless parade of prompting me from one place to another.

"Coming! Just a minute!" I yelled, trying not to sound too irritated.

I dusted myself off and pulled out my rain boots. I doubted they'd be warm enough, but they were an improvement over the wet Vans. Fancy Beast was perched on the back of the chair, looking out the window at the lake. She let out a tiny meow as I grabbed my phone.

"Be good today." I told her, as if she had evil plans.

I ran downstairs and into the kitchen to pour myself a cup of coffee. Mom was baking muffins.

"Those rubber rain boots aren't going to work in this snow. Your feet will freeze..." Mom was mid-sentence when I exploded.

"Well what else am I going to wear!? It's snowing outside and my Vans got soaked." I was prone to impulsive rages, especially when I felt criticized.

"A-hem. I wasn't finished with my sentence." Mom, an expert in my moods, remained calm in the face of my mini-fit. "As I was saying, look on the table and see what I got you. And *you're welcome.*" Mom shook her head and drank a giant swig of coffee.

I really needed to practice my self-control. I drank a few sips of coffee and picked up the box on the table. A pair of fur-lined Sorel boots, in a dark grey.

"They are super warm and great for the snow and slush." Mom plopped blueberry muffin mix into silicone cupcake molds, licking her fingers.

I heaved off my rain boots and put on the Sorels. Now I knew why everyone had a pair. My feet felt instantly warmer and cozy.

"Thanks Mom. I'm sorry. I didn't mean to yell. It's just..." I hugged her with one arm and smiled guiltily.

"I know. I know. Now go, you're going to miss the bus." Mom pointed to the clock on the wall, smirking.

I quickly sprung to action like a black-and-white cartoon character with action lines pulsing off around it.

"Bye!" I was out the door.

It was two blocks to the school bus stop. I walked slowly as I paid attention to everything around me. These curious little bluejays, with vivid blue bodies and majestic crested black heads, squawked at the squirrels, who chirped back with force. Some of the squirrels here were different; they had these little tufts on their ears and it was adorable. They chased each other up and down the big pines, their nails scratching loudly on the bark. I found myself smiling as I walked, watching the squirrels race up the tree in a circular sprint to the top. I stopped in my tracks. Wait, was I smiling? I shook my head laughing to myself. Moods. The bus pulled up to the stop, and I hurried the last twenty feet to get to the open door, my backpack jingling as I bounced along the snowy pavement in my new boots.

The bus was heated inside and it was really warm. Too warm. My cheeks tingled and stung as I leaned against the freezing window trying to find a temperature balance. There was still snow on the ground and some freezing rain expected today.

The bus curved its way to school; it was loud and smelled of diesel and cheap vinyl. Suddenly, the horrible-sounding bus brakes squeaked to an abrupt halt. I strained my neck to see what was going on. In the road was a protest; I could see people holding NO FRACKING signs and similar homemade signs. One read WWW GO HOME! The bus driver inched along as the protestors slowly moved aside, allowing us to get through. I watched the faces of the people holding the signs, angrily chanting slogans. A local news van was interviewing some locals. The bus finally got through and we were on our way.

Maybe ten other kids were on the bus with me, but I didn't know any of them. Some chatted with each other, others sat alone like me. Quiet. Texting. I was usually too tired in the morning to try to talk to anyone. My phone vibrated. Robin sent a selfie from the beach. Tongue stuck out, peace sign displayed.

SoCal misses you! 🤍

I snapped a picture from the bus, the window foggy, showing the snow topped trees.

Currently bus sick and freezing. 🥶

The bus brakes squeaked angrily again as we came to a painfully loud stop. The doors flew open aggressively. I tucked my phone in my pocket and made my way to school. Today, I was invited to lunch. I felt nervous. *What if I can't think of anything to say? What if Ethan's friends are boring? Iris seemed ok.*

Open mind. Open mind. This was my mantra as I climbed the school steps.

11:37AM. I sat in Ms. Erdo's literature class staring up at the standard school clock on the wall. Less than an hour until lunch. Ms. Erdo was breaking down Hamlet to us, and although I kind of liked Shakespeare, I had already read it last year. My mind was drifting as I doodled on my notebook. I was drawing the eye of the mountain lion, when a folded-up note in the shape of a fox head landed on my desk. I smashed my hand on it, palm down, and looked slowly behind me. A student in the back corner was looking right at me. Maybe I saw them before with Ethan but I couldn't remember. She, *he?* was wearing fuzzy fingerless animal paws, like gloves and what looked like hand made animal ears on top of their head. Probably a fox? A spunky looking Korean girl or maybe a boy? I wasn't entirely sure, and it didn't entirely matter. They pointed to the note. I turned back around and quietly unfolded the note, trying not to be heard.

I'm Terra. From Ethan and Iris's pack of pals.
I hear you're joining us for lunch today.

Welcome.

Here's a quiz:
1. Twix or Reeses?
2. Sun or Rain?
3. Pineapple on pizza?
4. Do you like to craft?
5. What is your favorite gemstone?
6. Pronouns?
7. Got any pets?

How spectacularly random! I looked back at Terra, who looked inquisitively back at me. I held up a just-a-minute finger, and got to work on my answers.

Hi Terra. I'm Anya.
Reeses all day long
Sun please
Pineapple on pizza but only with Pepperoni
I don't really craft much — although I'd like to start.
I like moonstones.
She/Her
A cat named Fancy Beast— age 4

I folded the note back up the way it was delivered to me and feebly tried to pass it back to Terra, except it ended up on the floor about two desks away from them. I was not smooth. They buried their face in their hands, obviously laughing. I turned back around for a second, hiding my mortification.

Ms. Erdo was writing on the dry-erase board some homework assignment about writing a poem in iambic pentameter. I turned back around and saw that Terra had my note in hand. But how? They hadn't moved. Terra saw my surprised face and crooked an eyebrow at me with a waggle of magical fingers. They laughed silently. They read the note and the scrunched face was a clear indication pineapple on pizza around here was definitely no good.

The bell rang.

Oh how I wish there were no bells.

Terra waited for me as I gathered up my books.

"Nice answers by the way. But the pineapple on the pizza. Questionable." Terra twirled their tail whilst watching me struggle to get my books sorted.

"I stand by pineapple on pizza. I'll even go as bold to say it works with jalapeños." I was standing now, ready to head to lunch.

"Blasphemy!" Terra was laughing as they tugged on my backpack strap. "Let's go, the pack is eager to meet you."

"Pack? Like animals?" I crooked my head, amused.

"100% , there's Ethan and Iris who you know. Jimmy and his boyfriend Felix. Faye and Lucy." Terra had huge dimples and their face was round and cheerful. One of those people who made you automatically smile upon seeing them.

I followed Terra through the hallway and out the building, through the quad, and to the cafeteria. The sky was undecided if it wanted to snow or rain, but it was definitely threatening something. Terra was walking quickly through the bitter chill, their tail swaying with their gait. They looked back to be sure I was following.

"Did you bring your lunch or do you buy it?" Terra inquired hopping over a rock with impressive agility.

"I bring it." I said matter-of-factly, trying not to slip on the icy slush.

"Solid choice, the cafeteria food is revolting. The taco boats are especially offensive."

The large glass doors opened to a huge cafeteria. The line for the hot food seemed to be moving swiftly. Several teachers looked tired; they were on duty to police the lunchtime chaos. *God, they wear whistles.*

I looked to the back near a long row of vending machines. Ethan was standing on his chair at the table waving at us and gesturing to come over. As I looked at the "pack" it was like stumbling upon a herd of deer in the middle of the night. All heads turned towards us and eyes staring. It was startling, but intriguing. I scanned the room looking at other groups of kids. I could see the ski and snowboarder crowd, the super pretty rich kids, some nerds, loners, stoners, brain rots, and some rock-climber types.

Ethan launched off the chair, almost in flight, to greet us.

"There she is! Come meet everyone." Ethan smiled wide, warming me from the inside out. I put my backpack on the back of a chair and waved close to my chest.

"Hi." I said shyly. I counted seven people.

"I have successfully delivered the new girl." Terra gestured much like the ladies on gameshows, motioning to cars, RV's and jet skis.

"OK, let's all go around the table and introduce ourselves to Anya. Then, Anya, it will be your turn to tell us about you." Ethan was like a host of a reality dating show.

Terra chimed in. "I'll go first. As you know, I'm Terra. I'm allergic to strawberries, I'm a Leo and I have no interest in dating. My favorite color is not invented yet and I have the wolf as a theriotype." Terra wagged their tail at the table.

"We're off to a good start, no one feed them strawberries." Ethan laughed.

"Please no." Terra sat down and removed a small paper sack lunch from their backpack.

Two guys stood up at the same time. One was very petite, with dark brown eyes, sporting black makeup shading all around his eye area. His hair was cut into a kind of a fluffy mullet.

"I'm Jimmy and this is my boyfriend Felix." Felix, an athletic-looking Black guy with green eyes, was a good foot taller than Jimmy. He nodded and smiled. Jimmy continued, "I love junk food and binge-watching movies. Felix and I have been together since sixth grade. I've lived on the lake my whole life. I've been told I have shamanistic qualities, whatever that means. Oh, and I can play the piano really well. My theriotype is the raccoon, and maybe some others, but mostly raccoons."

"Theriotype? So all of you have like, a favorite animal?" I asked, naively.

"It's a little more than that." Felix smiled. "But, yes. Like Jimmy said, I'm Felix. I also have lived in Emerald my whole life. I'm an expert on '80s music. Ask me anything! My theriotype is the deer. And I read tarot cards for a side hustle. My YouTube channel, DeerFelixKnows-ALL, just hit 100,000 subscribers." The table all did a little 'pump it to the ceiling' dance.

"He's so good. And he often buys us pizza, WITHOUT PINEAPPLE, with all his influencer cash," Terra smirked.

"This is true." Felix sat down, index finger to the sky.

Iris was eating a banana and with a full mouth said. " I don't wanna stand up. Do I have to stand up?"

"No Iris, you can share your fun facts sitting." Ethan smiled.

"We met already. I'm Iris. I moved here last year from Portland, Oregon. I met these wonderful weirdos and now I'm exactly where I belong."

"Do you wanna share your theriotype?" Jimmy asked.

"Oh right.. sorry, my ADHD." Iris chuckled. "Fox. I am definitely a fox." Iris dug through her lunch, looking displeased at certain items. "I think we're pretty much all neurodivergent. My guess is many therians are, because all our senses are heightened—just like the animals."

Lucy removed her noise-canceling headphones, similar to mine, but hers were customized with little tiny tufted ears.

"Squirrel?" I pointed at Lucy curiously.

"Yes! Well done, Anya. I'm Lucy. I've lived here for two years. I came here from San Francisco. I love to code and create games online. I'm trying to build a game that connects people to nature and creates awareness for recycling. I'm working that in as part of the gameplay." Lucy plopped down in her seat and put her headphones back on. Her brown hair was cut in a tight bob; she wore bright pink lipstick and an oversized sweatshirt. She was really tall.

"Wow, that is impressive." I said. Lucy smiled and nodded.

"Yeah, Lucy is pretty much a genius." Felix chimed in as the table all nodded in agreement.

Ethan jumped on the table like he was surfing on it, and double finger pointed at the last member of the pack. "Last but not least....Faye!"

The nearby teacher blew a whistle, rattling my last nerve and disturbing pretty much everyone.

"Sloan. Off the table." Coach Brendan yelled. Ethan jumped off quickly.

Faye stood up. "Well, that was unpleasant and unnecessary. I'm Faye. I've lived here my whole life, I won't eat popcorn or anything with seeds. I just broke up with my boyfriend. Don't ask me about that. Like Jimmy, I eat a lot of candy. I'm a Capricorn and my theriotype is the bear." Faye was all business. She had black long hair, similar to mine, and big dark brown eyes. She was wearing a black Dickies coverall and ketchup colored Doc Martens. She had a tattoo on her forearm of a bear paw with scratch marks coming off the claws. I don't know if it was real or fake, but it looked legit.

Ethan, the obvious leader of the group, walked over to me holding a pretend microphone to my mouth.

"OK, I'm Anya. I obviously just moved here. My parents got divorced and so we moved back to where my mom grew up. She's half Tuhánee..."

"Oh, I'm Tuhánee too." Jimmy interrupted.

"Oh cool." I smiled. "I have a fat cat named Fancy Beast. I miss my best friend Robin, who is one of the funniest people I know. I grew up in Hollywood and now I am here." I sat back down and opened my Bento box with my lunch. I wasn't hungry, but I started eating carrots.

"You're from Hollywood?" Lucy asked. "Did you see celebrities and stuff?"

"Yeah. Sometimes. You know, at the grocery store and like, Runyan Canyon. I saw Billie Eilish at Lassens once." I reported.

"Cool. What's Lassens?" Faye asked.

"It's a health food store." I replied. "Hey Ethan, what's your theriotype?"

Ethan spread his arms out to the side as wide as he could reach. "The eagle." He boasted.

"That tracks." I laughed. The bell rang. Everyone hustled to shove food in their mouths and collect their gear. Ethan looked at Terra, who nodded affirmatively.

"Anya, we're all hanging out this weekend. We're going on a hike. There will be pizza. Do you want to join us? We'll meet at my place. I can text you the address?" Ethan was walking backwards towards the doors. Everyone was pouring out of the cafeteria, heading to their next class.

"That sounds great, yes. Thank you." I rushed out the doors with the mob. I guess I passed the test.

3

ANY DREAMS?

The school bus rattled away, leaving me in a cloud of exhaust. I coughed, horrified this toxic relic was still on the road, ruining the mountain air and my lungs. As I walked the two blocks home, I saw the same squirrels playing chase up a sugar pine. I stopped at the tree, looking up from the base. My neck craned, and I felt a flash of vertigo from the sheer height. Stepping back with my palm pressed against the wet bark I breathed in deeply, feeling calm. The two squirrels chattered down at me.

"Hey guys, want some snacks?" I rummaged around in my backpack, pulling out a baggie of trail mix I hadn't had time to eat. I picked out the M&M's, eating them, as I made a little pile of nuts at the base of the tree. The two squirrels looked down at me, waving their tails from side to side. I took about five paces back, waiting to see if they'd come down. They just stayed on the branch, vocalizing. After a few minutes I lost patience and started walking home. I looked back and, sure enough, the squirrels were feasting.

The door to the cabin was unlocked and I walked in, dropping my backpack. The fireplace was lit and I smelled coffee. I could hear Mom talking to someone in the kitchen.

"Anya, is that you?!" Mom yelled from the kitchen.

"Yeah," I yelled back. I made my way to the kitchen; I could hear Mom talking. I held back to eavesdrop. An older woman was speaking. "No one can believe it, but it passed. I don't know what dirty business went down, but all of a sudden, all the Ganns and the Stevenses and that crowd, the quote-unquote 'old Lake families' were all for it, and with all their connections to the city council and the legislature, next thing you know it passed by one vote. The backers are all a bunch of Silicon Valley tech bros, and who knows how much money they have or who they bribed with it."

"What?" Mom laughed in disbelief. "Fracking? Here? Tech bros? Auntie, you're joking." Mom sounded unconvinced.

"Get this," the older woman said, "the company is called Well, Well, Well, LLC."

"That's tech bros all right," Mom said wearily. "Ugh."

"It's a real mess. The balance needs to be restored, or you know what will happen." The older woman warned.

"Stop," Mom said abruptly. I decided this was my opportunity to breeze in. "Hi!" I walked in, fresh. Mom was pouring coffee. At the table sat an older woman.

"Anya, this is your great-auntie Lily." Lily stood up, looking at me with awe. "Anya." She smiled wide, revealing a shiny gold front tooth. She was very petite, with salt-and-pepper hair back in a bun. She had hooded eyes and chiseled cheekbones. She was looking really good for seventy-four. Lily walked up to me and cupped my face in her rough, arthritic hands. "You look like your grandmother Mae, and your mother." Lily was delighted.

"Oh, hi, Auntie Lily. It's nice to meet you." I smiled and reached out with an awkward hug. She was so little I was afraid I would break her.

"How was school today?" Mom's standard question.

"Yeah, OK. The bus got stuck in a protest but we still made it in time. I had lunch with Ethan and all his friends. They are really nice. Different, but nice."

"Auntie Lily came by to meet you, and she's staying for dinner," Mom announced.

"Oh that will be nice." I said in that polite tone, the way you do when you talk to old people and don't know what else to say. "I'm going to go up to my room and do some homework and rest. Will you call me when dinner is ready? I'm so tired." I was worn out. All the moving and newness just had me wrecked.

"Sure, sweetheart. Take a nap." Mom smiled. Auntie Lily squeezed my hands. "We'll call for you later."

Relieved I didn't have to make small talk, I walked upstairs and closed the door to my room. I thought about the conversation I overheard. Fracking. I knew that was bad. I'd ask Ethan later about it. In my room, Fancy Beast was fast asleep on the back of the chair. I opened the door and went out on the deck, standing, looking over the massive lake. My breath was visible from the cold. A lightning bolt cracked off in the sky some distance away, followed by a rumble of thunder. *That's weird*, I thought. *Does lightning usually happen in a snowy winter?* I thought of thunderstorms as more of a warm-weather thing. I didn't know enough about snowy weather to say, but it was unsettling.

I heard a whooshing noise, and a bald eagle flew by close enough that we locked eyes. His wingspan was massive. My God, that was a huge bird. I saw hawks all the time in Los Angeles, but never bald eagles. I thought about Ethan, and pictured him with his arms outstretched, emulating the eagle. Theriotype. I needed to Google that. I mean, I know what they meant, but it was a word I had never heard before today. This pack, they were so welcoming and kind. I wasn't really sure why they picked me to hang out with them, but I was grateful to make friends. I had felt so lonesome since moving.

There was something about these new friends that felt familiar on some level, yet totally foreign. I couldn't quite figure it out.

My eyes refused to stay open. I came in from the cold, closed the door, and took off my boots, laying them near the heating vent to dry off. I climbed on my bed and pulled my weighted blanket over me. The clock read 4:00 p.m. exactly. I turned off my phone and felt so deliciously comfortable. Sleep, glorious sleep. Within seconds, I heard the buzzing. My body vibrated and crackled. The green glow was all around as I floated above myself. *"Focus, Anya,"* I thought. I could see Fancy Beast fast asleep on the chair, the clock on the night-stand, everything in the room where it belonged. I lay peacefully on my side, yet here I was, totally aware of everything. I thought about the library, and within an instant I was standing in the familiar room, books everywhere, with the fireplace roaring. Frederick was sitting by the fireplace in a large tufted red velvet chair.

"Anya, you're getting closer to your purpose. Stay the path." Frederick smiled at me.

"But what does that mean? What purpose?" I asked, as I walked closer to him. The mountain lion figures loomed almost as tall as me, fierce yet serene.

"You're exactly where you belong." Frederick stood up and walked towards the bookshelves. He vanished, and I was alone in the library. I turned towards the statues and touched the top of the mountain lion's head. As I did, my entire body shook with chills. The chills pulsated through every inch of me, but it felt incredible, a feeling I had never experienced before. My hand was tingling and hot, but once again nothing was uncomfortable. My eyes locked with the mountain lion's, and the blue glowed so brightly I had to look away. I felt myself hurl backwards into space, moving at impossible speeds.

I was back in the bedroom, but still not awake. Everything was as it had been. I looked out the window at the lake, and was startled as I saw Ethan standing on the deck outside my window. He had the eagle on his arm and was looking in the window at me, smiling. That startled me awake. I sat up in bed with my heart pounding so hard, shaking. I looked at the clock. 4:27 p.m. Time was playing tricks on me. 4:27?? I felt like I had been asleep for hours. I looked out on the deck, but no one was there. A lightning bolt exploded into a multitude of bolts and shot across the sky, reflecting on the lake. The thunder chased the lightning in quick succession. Fancy Beast jumped off the bed and went underneath it. I thought about the mountain lion statues, and the minute I did, I felt that same energy pulse through me. It was so pleasurable and weird—exhilarating was the right word. I sat with my face in my hands. What was going on? I was still so tired. I rolled over and fell asleep.

My alarm went off, but I was slow to stir. The sun was rising, and the fog and gloomy clouds were hovering over the lake. My room was dark. I was still in yesterday's clothes. I slept the WHOLE NIGHT!? I sprang out of bed, panicked. Fancy Beast was annoyed I was disturbing her. She would prefer I just stayed in bed 24/7. I looked at my phone to confirm it really was the following day. I hurried to the shower and got ready pretty quickly, for me. I could smell bacon and eggs cooking. Ohhh, it smelled so incredible. I walked down the stairs, Fancy Beast in tow. The kitchen was warm and had its own fireplace, which was lit and crackling. Mom was standing at the island, cooking eggs.

"Well, look who's up." Mom smiled.

"Why didn't you wake me last night? I thought we were having a dinner with Auntie Lily?"

"You were so out of it. I tried to wake you but you needed to sleep. Auntie Lily understood. We had a nice dinner and caught up. She's teaching me how to make the Tuhánee baskets. I thought I could earn a little extra income. Her hands are getting so bad with the arthritis, she isn't able to keep up with her orders. So I was going to take over." Mom seemed optimistic.

"Oh, for Dan Gann the Souvenir Man?" I laughed.

"Oh geez, not that guy." Mom made an ick face.

I had overheard her and Dad talking, and I knew they were fighting over alimony and child support. I didn't know how the lawyers were working it out, but I could tell Mom was stressed. She had never worked since having me, so being on her own now was probably scary.

"These baskets are Tuhánee art, right?" I picked one up that was in the middle of the table, holding napkins. Mom nodded and brought over a plate of eggs, bacon, extra crispy, some toast and orange slices. She knew I was hungry after not having dinner.

"Yes. Our tribe is known for these baskets, and I used to be really good at doing them when I was about your age, but it's been so long. Auntie Lily is refreshing me on how to keep them authentic with the designs and patterns. They actually sell for good money." Mom was pleased. Aunt Lily sells them to the gift shop at the Native American Museum. You know, where they sell *actual* Native American art."

"Mom, how come you never tell me anything about being Tuhánee?"

"What do you want to know?"

"I don't know." I shrugged. "It just seems like you were taught traditions and stuff and I don't know anything."

"I left here a long time ago and I kinda wanted to leave a lot behind. When I met your dad, and we had you, I just felt like a different person. I wasn't ashamed of being Tuhánee, but the traditions and legends here... " Mom trailed off.

"Yeah?" I nudged.

"You better get going to school." Mom seemed bothered. I knew her well enough to know not to press her on this, so I changed the subject.

I scarfed my breakfast and broke off a little bacon for Fancy Beast, who was harassing me for treats. I drank two cups of coffee. Mom handed me my lunch, and I was ready for another exciting episode of "Ride This Craptastic Bus to School."

"Mom, I was invited to hang out with Ethan and all his friends this weekend. I guess he's having everyone over for pizza and a hike." I mentioned, as I re-tied my bootlaces.

"Oh that sounds really nice, Anya. I'm so glad you're making friends. I can drop you off," Mom said with a sigh of relief.

"Yeah, I don't know where he lives yet, but I'll let you know." I grabbed my backpack and rushed out the door. "Bye!"

Sitting in Ms. Erdo's literature class, I was lost in my drawings. I usually liked school OK, but I felt like everything I was learning here I already knew. I hated to waste my time relearning things, so I was checked out. Luckily, I was a great test-taker, so my grades usually worked out, considering the amount of effort I put in. Mom said I was lucky to be so smart, but not to use that as an excuse not to stay curious.

Terra was sitting behind me today and handed me another note, this one a rabbit.

"Another quiz?" I whispered. Terra nodded with that infectious smile. I unfolded the origami rabbit and inside found just one question.

Did you have any dreams last night?

I looked at the words staring up at me. Why did they ask me that? It was creepy, as if they knew something. I scanned over the dream in my mind and remembered seeing Ethan looking in the window at me, with the eagle perched on his arm. I started to feel sweaty and nervous. Why are they all trying to be my friend so fast? My paranoia was off the charts. I had never told anyone about the dreams, not even Robin. I stood up abruptly and walked out of the classroom, heading to the bathroom. The lunch bell was set to ring in five minutes. I couldn't wait. Ms. Erdo shot me a look of annoyed concern as I walked out of the room.

I sat in the toilet stall, trying to calm my breathing as my mind raced. What was real? Was I overreacting? I had a tendency to do that. The bell rang, echoing through the tiled bathroom. I slammed my hands over my ears to block the sound. I looked up at the ceiling and pondered why people threw spitballs. With the lunch bell, the bathroom became flooded with students. So many people. The pretty girls gossiping and touching up their makeup, fixing their hair, peeing, and what have you. I just sat in the stall, frozen, wishing for peace. I didn't want to come out. I didn't want to see Ethan and everyone at lunch. I slipped out of the bathroom when the noise died down and went to the library. It was quiet there. No one would bother me. I put on my headphones and played ocean wave sounds as I doodled in my notebook.

The chair next to me moved back and Ethan sat down.

"Hey." he whispered. "Are you OK?"

I took off my headphones and looked deep into his eyes, searching for something.

"I don't know. I don't know anything." I replied quietly.

"I know things. I know that you're Tuhánee. I know you get the visions. I know your mom had them too." Ethan did seem to know a lot of things.

"What are you talking about?" I said a little louder now, defensive. "You don't know my mom."

"My dad does. Anya, it's a small town. He told me about her." Ethan smiled gently.

"Told you what?" I was angry.

"I'm not a bad guy. I'm your friend, or, I want to be. We all want to be. You're like us. Come, tomorrow. We can explain." Ethan put his hand on my hand trying to reassure me.

"Like you?" I was so confused. "Look, I don't have a theriotype," I snapped.

"No?" Ethan said, with obvious disbelief. He looked at my notebook, filled with drawings of the mountain lion's eyes. Ethan took my pencil and wrote an address down under the drawings. Then he wrote: *noon —tomorrow*. He got up and, with a wink, walked out of the library.

I sat staring at the doodles. I turned page after page filled with drawings of mountain lions. I didn't realize how many drawings I had done. It was just stream of consciousness in action. I put Ethan's address into my phone contacts. I was freaked out, but curious.

4

THE THERIANS

I was quiet on the drive over to Ethan's. Mom seemed cheerful I was having a social interaction; it relieved the guilt she had for moving me away from everything I loved.

It was starting to lightly snow as we twisted along the mountain road, and I stared out the window, thinking about what Ethan had said about Mom. I wanted to ask her about it, but I decided to just see what happened today. The car slowed to a stop as we approached Ethan's house. It was set back from the street and more remote than our place. Our place was on the lakefront, so we have neighbors all around us, but this home felt tucked into the trees, a large mountain looming behind. Ethan came outside when he saw our car. He gave a huge smile and waved, and Mom went white as if she had seen a ghost.

"Is that Ethan?"

"Yeah. Why?" I asked.

"Ethan Sloan?"

"Yes Mother, Ethan Sloan." I was gathering my backpack and had one foot out of the car. Ethan came over, and true to his nature, started talking to Mom.

"Hi, Anya's Mom! I'm Ethan." He was charming.

Mom just stared at him in disbelief. "Is your dad Luke Sloan?" She asked, almost seeming afraid to know.

"Sure is. Wanna come say hi?" Ethan offered. "He's right inside."

"NO, uh no. I have some Zoom meetings, uh yes, I have some Zoom meetings so I have to hurry back. But Anya, have fun. Call me if you need a ride later."

"You don't Zoom." I accused. Mom shot me a look. "I Zoom now." I closed the car door and followed Ethan to the house. I looked back to see Mom just watching us, completely frozen. Then, as if she had come to her senses, she backed out of the driveway and drove off.

"Is she OK?" Ethan asked.

"I actually don't know. She is acting so weird." I laughed in that annoyed embarrassed way parents make you feel.

"Parents are weird." Ethan smiled that glorious smile. "Come on, everyone is in my room."

Ethan's house was warm and inviting. It wasn't so much of a cabin vibe like ours, but more of a traditional mountain A-frame with a large deck in the front of the house and massive windows from floor to ceiling. Inside a big orange wood-stove fireplace was burning. This place had a really fun 1970s feel to it, complete with a lava lamp and shag carpeting. I don't think I had ever seen shag carpeting in real life.

"Come on, my room is up here. I'm glad you decided to come." Ethan took my backpack for me.

"Is that shag carpet?" I asked, totally intrigued.

Ethan laughed out loud. "Welcome to the time capsule. My Dad is obsessed with the 1970s, if you can't already tell. He even has a waterbed and an oil rain lamp in his bedroom."

"I don't even know what that means." I admitted, as we started up the stairs. Ethan's dad came in from the kitchen.

"Ethan, are you making fun of my fantastic style?" A voice boomed.

"Style?" Ethan mocked.

"It's so out it's in. I keep telling you that." Luke said with conviction.

"Right." Ethan poked back.

"Anya?" Luke asked inquisitively. Luke Sloan was tall and very handsome. He looked a lot like Ethan, but just more relaxed, and obviously older. Ethan could be so hyper, where his dad seemed really mellow.

"Yes, I'm Anya." I smiled. Luke shook his head.

"Wow, you're the spitting image of Mary, uh, your mom." He looked at me like he was trying to figure something out.

"Dad, we're going upstairs. We're going onto the trails later." Ethan interrupted.

"Yeah, OK, be careful." Luke looked at me a little longer. "It's nice to meet you." He walked back to the kitchen, and as I watched him, I noticed he had the same walk as Ethan.

As we entered Ethan's room, I was feeling nervous, especially after running out of literature class. Ethan's bedroom was big, with a huge bed on a platform, several bean bags, and some long tables with loads of art supplies. There was a sea-foam green Stratocaster guitar hanging on the wall, and a snowboard in the corner of the room. Mounted above his bed a huge, beautiful black-and-white photograph of a bald eagle.

The entire pack was hanging out, and everyone was busy crafting. Iris had a needle and thread and seemed to be doing a repair job on a fox tail. Terra was felting a wolf mask that looked incredible. Jimmy and Felix were sitting back to back on the floor. Jimmy was creating a raccoon makeup look with a handheld mirror, while Felix was painting a deer mask.

I looked around the room in awe. Everyone was so focused and talented. Faye had a full bear suit she was sewing. Lucy was eating trail mix and drawing.

Terra looked up first and saw me watching everyone with wonder. "Hey Anya. I didn't mean to upset you with the note."

"I tend to overreact." I said embarrassed.

"I think we all have that problem." Iris laughed.

Ethan interrupted, "I wanna eat pizza. Felix!" Felix laughed and got on his phone. "Fine, I'll order it. The usual, Cheese?"

"YES." everyone said in unison.

"Anya, sit with me. Here, draw something." Lucy handed me a sketchbook. I took the notebook and started sketching. There was a very harmonious feeling to just sitting together and being creative. We were connecting to one another without even speaking. Ethan had some music playing and everyone was just in their zone. It was almost meditative.

Full of pizza and sodas, we all walked outside to start the hike. The weather was cold. A storm was brewing, and I could see my breath as I put on my gloves. Felix and Jimmy were holding hands as they strolled with ease. Terra was racing ahead with Faye and Ethan. I was lingering behind with Iris and Lucy. The trail started behind Ethan's house and inclined uphill. The snow was pretty powdery, so it was easy to maneuver. One thing I liked most about the snow was how quiet it made everything. All the sounds of the world just got absorbed into the fluffy snow, leaving an eerie, yet wonderful silence. But just as I was blissfully enjoying the silence, the ground shook slightly.

"Whoa. Did we just have an earthquake?" I was well versed in quakes.

"Yeah, a manmade one." Lucy scoffed.

"Some idiots are trying to get some natural gas in these mines outside of town. They just started fracking recently." Iris was disgusted.

"Oh, I saw the protest about that, and all those signs. So what is fracking, exactly?" I asked.

"They basically fracture or "frack" the bedrock and shoot liquid in the holes trying to expand and crack the Earth up, to get more oil or gas. When they pump it out, there are all these huge voids that have nothing supporting them, and you get these weird earthquakes. I don't think they know what they're doing." Lucy said, sadly. We all fell a little silent.

"That sounds bad." I said.

"Yeah, it's not good. The politicians gave the OK to do it and this brand-new company just set up and started recently. I kinda wanna go check it out, but it's like a fortress," Ethan stated, depressed.

The mood dropped. No one was rushing, and the hike was pretty easy as we went deeper into the forest on a steady incline. The pines were massive, and the boulders were topped with fresh snow from last night's storm. I picked up some impressive pinecones along the way.

There was a circular clearing ahead, and as we approached, everyone seemed to get excited. Ethan was running and throwing snowballs at Terra. Lucy, Terra and Iris started running all around the clearing, but on all fours and really fast. It was insane.

"Whoa, that is wild!" I yelled, laughing in amazement.

"They're practicing their quadrobics," Jimmy enlightened me.

"Quad what?" I asked, completely naive.

"Quadrobics. It's quadrupedal movements like trotting, cantering, jumping and crawling. Basically, emulating animal movements." Felix informed me.

I had never heard of such a thing. I watched in awe as they jumped and raced with one another through the snow, so agile and fast, looking much like the animals they connected to.

Ethan was arranging some rocks into a circle around what seemed to be an already prepared fire pit. He got some sticks and wood from his backpack and was making a fire. He pulled out a lighter and got the fire going. I walked over to the fire pit and held my hands out to feel the heat.

"This is our spot, Anya. We come here all the time. It's like our secret hangout." Ethan smiled. "What do you think?"

"I think it's beautiful." I looked around at all the gorgeous trees and towering Sierra Nevada mountains. It felt so remote. Special. Everyone came over to the fire to warm up.

"Anya, we want to tell you something important. About us." Terra looked serious for once, and I could feel a nervous sensation spread across my chest.

"I think you know we all have a special connection to the animals. We are what you call therians or alterhumans. We relate deeply to certain animals and it's not something we have chosen but more like... they've chosen us."

"So your theriotypes are the animals you identify with, correct?" I asked.

"Yes, some of us are polytherian, meaning we identify with more than one animal, but most of us have been strongly connected to a certain animal." Terra stated.

"We think there's something bigger going on here. We all feel you didn't move to Emerald Lake by accident. I have been having dreams, or visions, for months about a girl who looked just like you. This girl holds a special place in the therian hierarchy. Like the missing puzzle piece. And we think that's you." Jimmy was rubbing his hands together over the fire.

"Is that why you guys have been so nice to me? What, you saw me coming?" I laughed nervously.

"You have visions, right? Super-realistic dreams?" Ethan looked at me, searching for my answer.

"How would you know any of that?"

"We're not trying to freak you out, just help you with your awakening." Iris said matter of factly.

"Awakening?" This felt like a weird intervention, but at the same time, everything they were saying was adding up with what I had been experiencing. Maybe they did know. Maybe this wasn't totally crazy.

"The awakening is when you first start to recognize your spiritual connection to the animals. It becomes a very intense experience. You have dreams. You have visions and you start to have encounters with your chosen animal." Faye said this with a warm smile.

I sat on a rock next to the fire, taking it all in. Just then, I heard a rustling through the trees behind me, and turned to look. A large black bear with three cubs was walking through the clearing. The mama bear stopped, her cubs playing with one another and tumbling around in the snow. My blood turned cold. I knew a mother bear could be extremely dangerous. And being a city kid, I had never seen a bear outside of a zoo. The entire group sat down at once and quietly watched the bears. Faye looked to be in a meditative state, smiling. Ethan saw my fear and whispered to me.

"It will be OK. Just stay quiet. Don't move." He reached for my hand slowly, squeezing it with reassurance.

The baby bears continued to play as the mother bear lumbered towards our group, very slowly. My breath quickened. The massive black bear flopped down in the snow, just sitting peacefully about ten feet from us. She watched her cubs play and kept a calm eye on all of us.

"What is happening?" I said to Ethan under my breath, so quietly I didn't think he would hear.

"Faye called her. It's OK. But remain calm," Ethan whispered back. "As our connections grow stronger, our abilities increase. The animals are reaching out to us. You are important in all this. We just have to listen." Ethan beamed. He closed his eyes and tilted his head to the sky. "Look up," He whispered.

It was hard to take my eyes off the bear, but I slowly tilted my head up and flying around the circle of trees was a bald eagle, its keek-keek call echoing off the mountains.

"Oh my God! Did you do that?" I caught myself talking too loud and sucked in a breath, as if to pull the noise back in. I watched the bears intently.

Ethan's hushed giggle answered my question. The eagle landed on top of the tallest pine and watched us below.

One of the baby bears ran over to us and sniffed at Iris. The mama bear stood up from her relaxed position. My heart actually stopped. I really think it just stopped and I was somehow dead. The baby bear wandered over to me, curiously sniffing at my backpack, probably smelling a package of cookies I had tucked away. Again, I assumed I had died minutes ago from sheer fear, but somehow my dead body was animated.

"Ethan, am I dead?" I whispered. I was so terrified I had no idea what reality was anymore.

"No, Anya, you are very much alive." Ethan said squeezing my shaking hand tighter. "Feel that?"

"Yes." I guess I wasn't dead yet. The cub stood on its hind legs and put its front paw on my shoulder, sniffing my ear. I didn't move. The baby bear was small in comparison to the mother, but the strength of this cub was apparent. The breath of the little bear was hot and tickled and vibrated my eardrum as he breathed heavily. I could feel the weight of his paws pressing on me. Mama bear was in motion, walking slowly and non-aggressively towards me. This was it. I was dinner.

Faye opened her eyes. "They're going to leave now. It's OK."

The mama bear walked right up to me and grabbed her cub. She turned with the cub in her mouth, tossing him in front of her, and headed back the way they all came into the clearing. They smelled so wild. Gamey. I was shaking and unable to stop. The bears all disappeared through the trees.

The pack all looked around at each other with huge smiles as hushed laughter turned to louder laughing.

"We still get so excited when they physically visit us." Felix said, elated.

"Wait so this happens like, on a regular basis?" I was shocked. I could barely speak.

"Yes. As we strengthen our connection to our animal counterparts we're able to communicate with them, ask them to visit us, like just now." Iris stated proudly.

"And we become more agile, our senses increase beyond what most humans possess." Terra informed me.

"Can you do it again?" I asked.

"Maybe you should try next time." Ethan encouraged.

"We can show you, Anya. We can help you." Faye walked over to me and crouched down at my feet. "You just have to fully connect with your theriotype."

I looked up through the circular clearing, at the vast mountain peeking in over us. The eagle was still standing on the branch, stars sparkling bright in the sky. I looked at him, and as I did he let out a cry, spreading his massive wings and taking flight over us.

5

WHAT STIRS BELOW

After returning from the clearing, most of the pack all made their way home. My phone had died, so I was charging it at Ethan's before texting Mom to come get me. I was sitting next to the big orange fireplace warming up. Ethan was walking Iris outside to say goodbye. A marshmallow on a stick was suddenly in front of me; I looked up and Ethan's dad was holding the offering.

"Can't really have a proper fire without toasting some marshmallows." He kneeled down in front of the fire, roasting his own.

"Thank you." I took the marshmallows and twisted them over the flame.

"How are you liking Emerald Lake?" Luke asked. His voice was so soothing. I liked his tone.

"It's different." I smiled.

"Different good or different bad?" He chuckled.

"Just different. I feel like I'm on Mars. It's beautiful, quiet, mystical somehow. It's so much quieter and calmer than Los Angeles, which I thought could be good for me. But I don't know. I can't tell yet. I miss

LA. I don't really do big changes well." The marshmallows were done, and I tapped my thumb and index finger over them to test the heat.

"Change can be scary. But, it also can be amazing. Sometimes you find yourself someplace new, and you realize later how that change affected the rest of your life, for the better." Luke said thoughtfully.

"Are you speaking from experience?" I asked eating the gooey marshmallows.

"Yes. I am. I wouldn't have Ethan if I never made a big change." Luke grinned.

"Can I ask a question? I haven't asked Ethan, but where is his mom?" I whispered licking sticky marshmallow goo off my finger tips.

"She lives in New York City, I think. We split up when Ethan was five. We met in college and got married young. When she got pregnant with Ethan, we moved back to Emerald. I wanted to raise Ethan here, but Ellie couldn't take the small town lifestyle." Luke ate his marshmallow.

"I'm sorry." I sensed sadness in Luke's voice.

"Me too. Ellie didn't know what she wanted, but she did know she wanted to party and be free. She wasn't very maternal. So after we split up, she tried to come back here and see Ethan, but the time became longer between visits. Eventually, she found some new boyfriend and went on the road with him. I'm not really sure where she is now. We haven't seen Ellie in about two years. She calls once in a while, but that's about it. Ethan seems OK about it, but I know it's not easy for him at times." Luke finished off his marshmallows.

I looked at my phone, which didn't seem to be charging. I fiddled with the plug and it started to charge.

"Shoot. My phone died. I thought it was charging all this time." I was exasperated.

Ethan bounced in the door. "It didn't charge!" I complained, holding up my phone.

"You can use my phone to call your mom to come get you." Ethan handed me his phone.

"Oh, let me just drive you home. The snow is starting to fall again pretty hard; I have the snow tires on. Save your mom from having to go back and forth." Luke offered.

"Yeah, I'll come along too," Ethan exclaimed.

"OK, that works." I gathered my things slowly and I put on my boots.

Luke and Ethan lived fairly close to us, and the road curving around the lake was a pretty drive.

"Up here, you just go left and then right," I instructed.

"I know where you live, Anya." Luke shot a knowing glance.

The snow was coming down harder, and the lights of the Bronco were shining brightly against the falling snow. The fog was getting thicker, and the effect was strange. Luke looked a little concerned. "Can't say I've seen fog with falling snow quite like this."

Up on the side of the road was a little surfeit of skunks waddling along. I instantly loved them. "We're supposed to get a bunch of snow tonight," Ethan warned. "I wonder if school will be closed tomorrow."

"Does that happen often?" I asked optimistically.

"Not too often, as the city keeps the roads plowed and salted, but if we get a real dump of snow sometimes they can't clear it fast enough," Luke informed me.

"Anya, do you snowboard?" Ethan asked, excitedly.

"Yeah. I have a board. I used to go to Mammoth and Big Bear with Robin. I'm not amazing, but I'm decent," I boasted. "Excellent!" Ethan was pumped. Luke slowed the car as we approached the cabin, turning into the driveway. Ethan hopped out of the car; Luke stayed in the car.

"Thank you, Luke," I said, gathering my things.

"You're welcome any time." He smiled that same warm smile of Ethan's.

I walked to the porch and Ethan grabbed my backpack, helping to carry it for me. I looked at Ethan as we stood on the porch.

"Today was wild," I laughed, thinking about the bears.

"It was great. I'm so glad you came over." Ethan looked at me with those blue eyes.

"Tonight, when you're drifting to sleep I want to help you with the visions. Before you go to sleep, let's try something. Say out loud 'I invite the eagle spirit of Ethan to join my vision.'" If you let me in, I can help you. Try this at 11:30pm, OK? I'll try to join you." Ethan looked at me with a serious expression.

"OK?" I said skeptical, but open. I mean, a family of bears hung out with us and we didn't become their dinner, so I guess Ethan might know what's what. "11:30. Maybe I'll see you." I smiled.

Just then the front door opened. It startled us. Mom was there, looking startled to see me.

"I was waiting for you to text me. Then I heard voices." Mom seemed surprised.

"My phone died so Ethan's dad offered to drive me home." I said.

"Good to see you again, Mrs. Petrova," Ethan said politely.

"Carlucci. I'm going back to my maiden name, but thank you and it's good to see you too." She still looked at Ethan wide-eyed. Mom turned her attention to the car in the driveway. The bright headlights from the Bronco made it impossible to see Luke in the car, and just then the car door opened. I heard Mom gasp quietly as she shaded her eyes.

Luke got out of the car and rested his arm on the car door. He squinted, and looked at us all on the porch, getting a better look at Mom.

"Hi Mary." Luke grinned like a kid on Christmas.

Mom took a step outside the front door onto the porch as though Luke was a magnet to her. She edged closer to the stairs, staring at him. Her face was showing a look I didn't quite recognize.

"Luke." Mom almost whispered. "It's been a while." Mary stood, motionless.

"It sure has." Luke sighed a good sigh. "You know, she looks just like you at fifteen." Luke shook his head in disbelief. Ethan was getting in the Bronco, and I was processing this awkward exchange.

"So I've heard." Mary smiled. Luke waved a gentle goodbye as he stood there a little longer. Then he got into the Bronco and backed out the driveway. I walked into the cabin, freezing, as Mom slowly followed behind me.

"So what was that? Were you flirting?" I said, including a distinct note of *I have busted you, Mother.*

Mom seemed light-years away.

"Mom?" I poked.

"We grew up together." Mom left it at that with a slight smile.

I didn't want to bug her about it, not yet. I tossed my bag next to the fireplace and went upstairs. Mom just followed me up the stairs and silently went into her room.

I ran a bath. I was still chilled to the bone, and I learned since being in Emerald the only real way I could get warm was to take a hot bath. The clawfoot tub was so big, and I absolutely loved taking baths in it.

I dropped a bath bomb in and watched the ball dissolve in fizzy aromatic goodness.

Fancy Beast sauntered in, taking a spot on the bath mat. The heater was humming along and I stood in front of the ancient vent, enjoying the hot air that pumped in. I put my hair up on my head and slid into the tub. The steam rising to the ceiling was clouding the antique etched mirrors. Next to the tub was a shelf with candles and dusty fancy soaps in a container. I lit one of the candles and let myself completely relax. There was a small window in the top corner of the bathroom, and all I could see was snow flying by it. A white assault of flakes swirling around. My phone chimed with a weird notification ding I didn't recognize. I picked it up and the banner read:

Inclement Weather Alert: Emerald and Pine Crest County Public Schools: School closures will be in effect for Monday.

Just then a notification came through from Ethan. He had added me to the pack's group Discord.

NO SCHOOL TOMORROW! SNOWBOARD? Party face emoji. The thread dinged with added happy and animal emojis from everyone. I added my own and smiled, feeling less lonely than I had in a while.

I was finally warm. I climbed into bed with full flannel pajamas and socks on, determined to stay toasty. My favorite weighted blanket was giving me all the calm feelings. Fancy Beast jumped up and squashed her fat butt next to me, in blissful cuddle mode.

Ethan wanted me to try this dream experiment at 11:30. It was almost time. I turned off the bedside lamp, and looked out my window at the snowstorm coming down. It was so beautiful. I felt myself getting more sleepy, Fancy Beast's purrs lulling me.

I took a few deep breaths. "I invite the eagle spirit of Ethan into my vision." I repeated this mantra over and over and over. As I was drifting to sleep I felt the buzzing begin. My entire body was electric. I felt the static and snapped right out of my body, floating above myself. This process was becoming less terrifying as I was getting more used to the sensations. I heard a voice in my head.

"Anya."

I somehow could see everywhere at once without having to try. Ethan was in the corner of my room. His voice wasn't really coming out of his mouth, but more like just appearing in my head.

"You're here." I was amazed.

"It worked," he replied. Ethan seemed to effortlessly float over to me, grabbing my hand. His touch felt more like energy vibrating than a flesh-and-blood hand. It was warm. He looked at me, and his glow was sparkly green like the rest of the room.

"Take me where you go." he instructed.

I thought of the library and Frederick, and within a millisecond we were both transported there. The fireplace was lit, the lions on each side, and the towering bookshelves as they always were. Ethan looked at the surroundings and touched the books on the shelf. He turned to me and looked so excited. He lifted a book off the shelf. It read *"Pathways."*

The same book! He flipped through it, pages gently fluttering.

"You brought a friend." Frederick was standing by the fireplace, twisting a ring off his finger.

"Yes, this is Ethan." I introduced him. "I don't know your name but I call you Frederick."

"Well how lucky, as Frederick is my name." He smiled charmingly.

Ethan was looking at the mountain lion statues by the fireplace. Frederick addressed Ethan. "And you are guiding Anya to her path."

Ethan smiled and replied, "I think so."

Frederick came closer to me than ever before. He held a gold ring in his hand, and he turned my hand over and placed it in my palm.

"For you." Frederick smiled and looked almost transparent. Once the ring was in my hand he dissolved into thin air. Ethan was standing by the lions.

"Come over here," Ethan asked, as I put the ring on.

I immediately found myself next to him and looking at the lions. "The mountain lion is your theriotype," he said.

"Look what happens when I do this." I touched the lion on top of its head and the eyes began to glow blue. "Ethan, look." A spectacular blue color filled the room. Ethan gasped with awe. "The mountain lion is the most powerful theriotype. It's the keeper of order and the strongest spirit animal, ensuring guardianship over the land." The same euphoric feeling took over as I placed my hand on top of the lion's head.

Ethan had an idea. "Place one hand on each lion head." I stretched my arms and was able to place my palms on the lions' heads. The sapphire of the ring was glowing. The second I had both hands on the lions, the light pulsated and erupted into an explosion of light, yet it was silent. The chills and euphoria doubled, and my body shook. Ethan looked concerned, but I knew I was OK. The book that Ethan had picked out of the shelf flew across the library and landed on the floor in front of us.

I lifted off the ground and was floating above the fireplace between both lions, the eyes still glowing, and now the statues were coming to life and shapeshifting into live animals. Ethan stared in complete shock. As the lions turned from marble to flesh I was slowly lowered between them. Both mountain lions nuzzled their heads under my hands as I scratched them affectionately; I felt my mind open and the feelings of the lions became a part of me.

Ethan looked over and squatted down to pick up the book. With that gesture, we were both thrown back out of the vision, and into our respective realities. I sat up in bed, heart racing. Fancy Beast, disturbed, was off the bed and hissing angrily. I looked around the room. Ethan wasn't there. On my finger was the ring. I turned on the light and inspected it. *How?* I thought. It was a gold ring with a relief sculpted on it of a mountain lion's head with a sapphire eye. I took it off, and inside it was engraved with my name. I placed the ring carefully in the nightstand drawer to keep it safe.

My phone dinged with a message from Ethan.

> We have a lot to talk about tomorrow. Can I come over?

> Yes!!

I put my phone on the nightstand. My body was tingling with the remnants of the euphoria I had with the lions. The storm was intense outside, but the wind was somehow soothing. Within minutes I was fast asleep.

Mom sat on my bed and gently shook me.

"Anya." Mom had a cup of coffee for me in her hand.

I was groggy, and so warm and comfortable. I hated to move. Snow was piled up on the deck to the window. The storm really dumped last night. I sat up in bed and took the coffee.

"Thank you." I croaked. "No school today."

Mom smiled. "I know, I got the notice. The good part about having actual seasons is you get a few snow days!" Mom patted my legs. "I'll make you some breakfast."

"What time is it?" I was disoriented.

"It's 8:30, sleepyhead." Mom laughed. She seemed back to herself after last night. She got up and scuffed her slippers down the hall. Fancy Beast jumped off the bed to follow her, expecting food.

As I sipped my coffee in bed, I opened the nightstand drawer. Yep, the ring was still there. I picked it up and examined it again, almost unsure if it was real. I turned it around and around in my hand, thinking about last night's vision.

I grabbed my phone and checked my messages. Nothing from Ethan had come in yet. I decided to clean out my closet after breakfast and unpack some of my boxes. I needed to find my snowsuit. Plus, I still hadn't really added anything from home to my room since the move.

Downstairs, Mom had made some oatmeal and fresh orange juice. I sat at the table, being warmed by the fireplace. I loved that we had a fireplace in the kitchen. It felt luxurious.

"Oatmeal is great snow day food." Mom chuckled.

"Is it OK if Ethan comes over?" I asked with a mouthful of food.

"Sure, that's fine. Auntie Lily might come over for a visit later." Mom said, making some tea. "I know she wants to get to know you."

"How come you never talked about our family before? My whole life I knew nothing about your Emerald life. And now we're here and it just feels weird." I searched Mom's face for anything.

"It's complicated. I still feel weird myself." Mom sighed.

"Then why did we move here? Why didn't we stay in LA, if being here is uncomfortable for you?"

"I told you, my options are pretty limited. Your dad left; the money part of that is still up in the air. You know I was a stay-at-home mom, so I haven't had any income all these years, and when everything went crazy with your dad and what's- her-face, I really only had this house to come to. I mean we have some money coming in from the sale of the LA house, but again, until your dad and I settle our divorce, I can't access those funds." Mom was worn out.

"I'm sorry." I said feeling guilty. "Would you sell this house?" I asked.

"No, I can't. Your grandmother left this to me as a life estate. Which means I can live in it, but I can't sell it. She did that specifically because she knew I would sell it if I had the chance." Mom was looking anxious.

"Would you have sold this place though, if you could?" I asked feeling somewhat sad at that prospect.

"Probably. I could get a fortune for this, right on the lake. We could have stayed in Los Angeles and lived well. But things didn't work out that way. Life rarely works out the way you think it will." Mom sighed. "Grandma Mae wanted this cabin to stay in our family forever, I guess."

"Well, it is special." I shrugged.

My phone dinged. It was Ethan.

Just woke up. Can I come over?

Sure.

I got up from the table. I walked over to Mom and hugged her tightly. She hugged me back in a way I could tell she needed. She held onto me so tight, and I knew just how hard this whole situation had been for her too.

"I'm so sorry Mom. I'm sorry I'm not a better daughter." I felt awful.

"Anya, what are you talking about? You're my world. I love you beyond anything else. None of this is your fault. You've been so good throughout all this upheaval. I wish things were different." Mom was teary. "I love you."

I reached out and squeezed her hand. I smiled, relieved.

"Ethan is coming over. I'm going to get dressed." I smiled.

"That's probably a good plan." Mom looked down at me in my pajamas and gave a little smirk.

I showered, and once dressed I ventured into my closet to go through some of the moving boxes. I pulled out some framed photos. One was of Robin and me at Halloween. It was a split frame showing us dressed like cats as fourth graders, and then last year, dressed as cats again. I smiled thinking about all the Halloweens we spent together. I pulled out my jewelry box, some awards from school, and a trinket box filled with all kinds of random junk. As I got lost in memories I just sat in the closet, zoning out.

"Hey!" Ethan poked his head into the closet, scaring me.

"Dude!" I yelled.

"Your mom let us in." Ethan laughed.

"Hi!" Jimmy was with him and poked his head around Ethan.

"Oh my God, Jimmy, hi!" I was happy to see the two of them.

"What are you looking for?" Jimmy asked. His face was always made up like a raccoon, which sounds cringey, but it was charming. It was just very Jimmy somehow.

"I'm not really looking for anything specific. Although I do need to find my snowboarding stuff, but I think those are in the garage. I'm just going through my moving boxes. I haven't unpacked much since the cabin is already furnished. There is so much junk in our garage, and I don't know what we're gonna do with everything."

Ethan looked behind me. "Wow, this closet goes way back." He started inching inside the closet with me.

"Yeah it has a little door—there is like, a mini-closet between the two bedrooms." I said.

"Oh Cool!" Jimmy exclaimed. "I wanna see." He was so small, he easily sneaked into the closet around Ethan and myself. Jimmy opened the small door. He turned on a light inside.

"I didn't know there was a light!" I said.

"Whoa, look at all these paintings." Jimmy was rummaging through them all. Ethan and I crawled into the small room, looking around at the newly-lit room.

Jimmy was sifting through the paintings, when one caught his attention. He stood, quietly looking at it. "What is it?" Ethan asked.

"Grandma Mae did these paintings, right?" Jimmy asked quietly.

"Yes, you knew Mae?" I was surprised.

"It's a small town. And we're both Tuhánee. I knew Mae. She was a great local artist." Jimmy pulled the painting out so we could see it. It was a rather large oil painting of the lake, always the lake. Coming up from the water was a creature that looked weirdly familiar. It was a winged animal with feathers and scales. The wingspan was huge. The face looked almost human and somewhat demonic and it had webbed feet. The creature was blasting out of the lake with great force. It looked menacing.

"Wait, what is that? Why do I know that?" I said, horrified.

"That is the Watanuuk." Jimmy said in almost a whisper.

Ethan looked on nervously.

"Hold on!" I gestured with both hands in the stop position. I rushed back into my room and opened my dresser drawer, where I grabbed the stuffed animal I got for Robin. As they clambered out of the small door, I shoved it at them and asked, "Is that, THIS?"

"What the heck!? Where did you get that?" Jimmy was rocking back and forth laughing.

"I got it at that souvenir shop. It was so hideous and weird I had to get it for Robin." I was pretending to make it fly.

"That is so ridiculous. I can't believe they have a stuffed Watanuuk. So you know the legend about it, right?" Jimmy asked.

"No, I didn't even know what it was. It was just so odd I had to have it." I laughed.

"My grandma used to say it lives in a nest at the deepest part of Oma'shélun, Emerald Lake. The Watanuuk is an old legend of the Tuhánee. Those that got too close to shore and had evil in their hearts were dragged to the nest, never to be seen again. The Watanuuk comes out when the balance of nature is off." Jimmy seemed worried thinking about it.

"Creepy! But that's like, fake, like Bigfoot or The Loch Ness Monster or something." I laughed.

"Bigfoot is real." Jimmy stated matter-of-factly.

"Yep, totally real." Ethan backed him up.

I looked at both of them seriously for a minute, waiting for them to share a Bigfoot sighting.

"Have you seen him?" I almost believed them. They both started falling over laughing.

"Fine, make fun of the city girl." I threw the Watanuuk at Ethan who dodged it with a terrified look on his face.

"Hey, I don't even sleep with my head in the direction of the lake, so you can laugh at me." Jimmy snorted.

"Wait, why?"

"My grandparents and their parents.. it's like just the way we do things. So sleeping with your head pointing towards the water leaves you vulnerable to the Eshooni and the Watanuuk." Jimmy was serious.

"Eshooni?" I squinted, confused.

"Auntie Lily or your mom never told you these things? They're Tuhánee legends." Jimmy rolled his eyes surprised.

"My mom never said anything about anything. And I don't even know Auntie Lily yet. Apparently she's coming over today." Ethan was examining the majesty of the stuffed Watanuuk, making faces at it.

"Ask Auntie Lily about the Eshooni. Apparently the Eshooni can bring people back to life. They live mainly in Cave Rock. It's a very spiritual place for our people. For the shamans." Jimmy smiled proudly.

"These are really different conversations then I had in Los Angeles." I laughed.

"So, last night." Ethan finally said.

I opened the nightstand drawer and pulled out the ring.

"Wow!" Jimmy was mesmerized. "That's cool."

"It came back with you?!" Ethan was shocked.

"Yea, when I woke up, it was on my finger." I said, bewildered. "Has that ever happened to you? Do things materialize from the dreams?"

"No, never. I mean not with me, at least." Ethan was still grasping this as he reached out to hold the ring. He turned it over in his hands and examined it.

"It's beautiful," Jimmy admired it and took it from Ethan.

"Ethan, you told Jimmy about last night, right?" I assumed. Ethan nodded. "Oh yeah. I told him."

Jimmy held up the ring. "Your theriotype is the mountain lion. Do you know what that means?"

"Maybe?" I said sheepishly.

"The mountain lion is so powerful. My grandma told me stories, and she said when a pack has come together and everyone is connected to their animal in unison, we can actually shape-shift." Jimmy exclaimed, giddy. "We've tried to do it, but we haven't had any luck. I think you might be our missing link." Jimmy handed me back the ring, which I placed into my drawer.

"What, like *turn into the actual animals?* How the heck does *that* work?" I blurted out.

"I don't know. The legends are real, though. But look, you have an actual ring from a vision, so there's that." Jimmy said.

"What *are* the legends?"

"My grandmother would always tell me these stories when I was little, before she died. Stories about the Eshooni that were in Cave Rock. They could cause illness or death but, like I said, they also can heal. It was the legend to go to Cave Rock to consult with the Eshooni, especially the medicine men."

"Cave Rock? Where's Cave Rock?" I had no idea.

"It's on the other side of the lake. It's kinda far from your place." Ethan said.

"Yeah, and women aren't supposed to go inside." Jimmy announced.

"Excuse me?" I was offended. "Did you just seriously say that out loud?"

"Well, I mean the legend is just for the medicine men to go in. I didn't make it up. I don't know, that was before they blew a hole in it, so maybe all bets are off." Jimmy said annoyed.

"Who blew a hole in it?" I was shocked.

"Take a wild guess, Anya." Jimmy, a professional at sarcasm, waved his right hand around in circles.

"Opportunistic white men?" I cringed.

"And the Trophy for Correct Super Obvious Answers goes to.... Anya!" Jimmy did a series of tiny golf claps.

"There's a road that goes through it now. Back in the 1930s, I think, they blew a hole in Cave Rock to put the road there." Ethan stated.

"Two holes, to be exact. They did a lot of bad things to Cave Rock. Legend is the Watanuuk came to restore balance. Apparently, it's come many times and it's never pretty. It kinda unleashes chaos with no real understanding of why. Just like a force of nature or something." Jimmy said in a hushed tone.

"Maybe we can talk to Auntie Lily. She may know more." Ethan suggested. "She knows all the legends. Maybe she knows about the ring too."

"Oh, Auntie Lily and my grandma were best friends. If anyone would know it would be her." Jimmy was excited.

"She's coming over later, if the roads are OK." I shrugged.

"Yeah the plows are out, the roads should be good soon." Ethan stated happily. "Jeez, does she still drive?"

"She drives a Mustang, dude." Jimmy laughed.

"Maybe she can help us. Or maybe your mom, Jimmy? Does she know?" I questioned.

"No, my mom is part Tuhánee, but she isn't really all that into the traditions and legends like my grandma. She's more into like, Louis Vuitton and her Range Rover." Jimmy laughed.

"We wait for Auntie Lily." Ethan announced.

6

SUICIDAL FISH

Jimmy, Ethan, and I walked out my back door onto the deck, and down the stairs to the pier. I had yet to explore the lakeshore since moving. The snow was so fresh and powdery, my hot breath showing in the cold air. The three of us walked out onto the old wooden pier. The sky had opened up and there was a super clear break in the cloud cover. It was gorgeous.

"The Tuhánee wouldn't walk on the shores or hunt alone." Jimmy stated. "They were afraid the Watanuuk would come get them, so they always came to the water in pairs or groups. Then they were safe."

"This Watanuuk is really scary," I shivered.

"It is." Jimmy confirmed. "I've been terrified of it my whole life."

"I'm more afraid of avalanches." Ethan made a distasteful face.

"Solid fear." I agreed.

"Do people swim in the lake or is everyone afraid of the Watanuuk?" I inquired.

"No one really knows about the Watanuuk but the Tuhánee and locals. That jerk-ball Dan used to sell Watanuuk t-shirts and I guess apparently now stuffed Watanuuks in his souvenir shack, but I'm not sure anyone really goes there, except you. I think it's a front for some money-laundering scheme."

"Like what?" I snorted. The idea this tiny souvenir shack could be a money-laundering front in this small town was hilarious to me.

"I don't know, it's just something my grandma said." Jimmy shrugged.

"Hmm. The guy that works there said something about Dan Gann selling stolen Indian artifacts out of the back of the store. He seemed to really hate the guy." I recalled.

"Somehow I don't doubt that. It tracks with Dan's reputation. More Watanuuk Fun Facts: It apparently lives in the middle of the lake, so I stay away from the center of Emerald Lake." Jimmy said.

Ethan chuckled.

"You keep laughing Ethan. But I've never seen you by the shore alone, or anywhere near the middle of the lake." Jimmy pointed at Ethan, his finger making little circles.

Ethan shrugged in agreement. "I don't mess with the legends."

At the end of our pier was a boathouse. It was locked, but we could peek in through the crack in the doors. Raised above the water was a red speedboat, looking disused and dusty, and on the walls of the boathouse were several wooden canoes hanging.

"Oh cool. We can have fun with this." Ethan was excited.

"Yeah, I don't think that speedboat works." Jimmy laughed.

"If the boat is broken, my dad can fix it. He can fix anything." Ethan bragged.

"Is that what he does?" I asked, curious.

"He's an architect, but he's good at fixing cars and things." Ethan smiled proudly.

We walked back from the boat house along the somewhat narrow pier. I heard a ruckus from the lake and we all looked back. A ton of bass were jumping out of the water, gasping for air, dying. We all stood staring at the weird behavior.

"Is that normal?" I asked, knowing nothing of bass.

"No." Ethan said. "I've never seen the fish do that."

"Okaaaay," Jimmy was perplexed. We just stood there watching the fish jump in unison up out of the lake and back under water. They did it over and over. They started jumping on the pier and we all ran off, avoiding the fish. We stood on the lakeshore, looking out at the weirdness. Then the ground began to shake. I thought it was in my head but as I looked at the cabin I could see it swaying side to side gently.

"What the heck is that?" I shrieked.

"I think it's those frackers. They're destroying everything!" Jimmy was horrified.

"This is bad." Ethan shook his head.

We watched the fish continue to fling themselves onto the pier, flopping helplessly.

"What is going on?" I asked. "The poor fish."

"I don't know, but the fracking has been going on a while, and the first quakes came about a month ago?" Jimmy looked to Ethan for confirmation.

"Yea. Everyone has been talking about it for a long time. They were trying to stop it, petitions and lots of meetings. They're still protesting. This isn't the place for something like that. It's been a big deal the last few years, but somehow, it got passed. Since the drilling started, things have been kinda odd. Like the weather and the animals are off." Ethan explained.

"Well, Well, Well LLC. - can you believe those guys? The audacity of that oh-so-clever name. People destroying our world with their arrogance, per usual. Sure, please, you haven't ruined Emerald Lake enough with the mining and the gold and the greed. Now fracking. Absolutely perfect." Jimmy yelled sarcastically to the sky, shaking his fist.

"My dad is worried they will cause really bad earthquakes. He thinks since they are doing it so close to the lake it could even wreck the lake somehow." Ethan said solemnly.

"Well, we have to stop them." I said, adamant.

"Or something will." Jimmy looked to the lake.

The three of us walked back up to the cabin, rattled. It seemed to get colder in the few minutes it took to reach the stairs. My hands were freezing.

"My mom has the fire going. Let's get warm. I'll make coffee." I smiled thinking of coffee.

"You're so addicted," Ethan teased. His smile doing that thing to my stomach again.

"I am *so* addicted," I agreed, laughing, my eyes sparkling, looking at Ethan.

"Get a room." Jimmy teased quietly, so only I could hear.

"What?" I objected in a protest whisper.

Jimmy nodded and made a little heart with his hands, pointing at Ethan's back.

"Stop," I mouthed, mortified.

The house was wonderfully warm. In the living room, laying across the couch, were my ski clothes, boots, snowboard and helmet.

"Oh cool! Mom found my snowboarding gear." I was delighted.

Ethan grabbed my board, inspecting it.

"Not bad, girl. Decent board." He approved.

We walked into the kitchen where I was about to make coffee. Sitting at the table alone, drinking tea and flipping through a magazine, was Auntie Lily.

"Anya." She greeted me with her glinting, gold-toothed smile.

"Hi, Auntie Lily. I didn't know you were here. These are my friends, Ethan and Jimmy. I'm gonna make some coffee, want some?" Aunt Lily raised her tea, showing she was covered.

"I know these boys. Jimmy, of course, and Ethan, you may not remember me too well, but I used to babysit you when you were about six." Lily smiled affectionately.

"You did?" Ethan strained to remember.

"You were very little and very wild. It was after your mom..." Lily let that sentence go. "Did you feel the shaking?"

"Yes. Is it the fracking, Auntie?" I asked. The boys sat next to Aunt Lily and I started getting the coffee in the grinder.

"I think so, yes." Lily looked defeated.

"Where's Mom?" I looked around.

"She's in the garage, going through boxes. It was too cold for me and I wanted to stay by the fire and drink some tea, and read my trashy magazine." Lily grinned. "Besides. You have questions for me, right?"

"How did you know that?" I asked, putting on the kettle.

"Sixth sense." Lily sipped her tea.

"Anya doesn't know any of the legends, Auntie. But she is very powerful." Jimmy explained.

"Of course she is. You all are. Anya, what is your animal? Has it picked you yet?' Auntie smiled slyly.

"Mountain lion." I said, warily, as I poured the boiling water into the French press.

Lily let out a small gasp, clasping her bony hands together. "The Mountain lion! I am the Elk." She said proudly.

Jimmy was surprised. "The Elk? That is the creation story of our people, Anya. The Elk brought us here to.."

"Oma'shélun," Lily finished Jimmy's sentence. "Emerald Lake."

"How does it work Auntie Lily? Can we really shape-shift?" I asked, skeptical.

"Yes. But you must all connect as a pack first. Under the half moon, which gives equal power to your two halves." Aunt Lily sipped her tea, slowly.

"You must all sit in a circle. The fire burns. You hold hands and call your animal spirits. Visualize them, ask them to join you. Thank them for coming. Always be thankful. They will come, and under the moonlight your powers as a pack will be unlocked for the transformation." Aunt Lily started to chant a little song.

"Oh, I know that song!" Jimmy was surprised, as if a core memory was unlocked.

"Jimmy, your grandmother taught you the chant. You remember it." Auntie Lily looked pleased.

Jimmy thought for a moment. "With the drum?"

"Yes, little shaman." Lily lit up.

"I remember it." Jimmy confirmed.

"You chant and play the drum. When they come, you will change. You will feel it." Lily made little circles with her tea cup, looking at the bottom of the cup."At least that's what the elders said."

"Do we need to be Tuhánee to shift?" Ethan asked.

"No, but you need to be called by the animals. If they have called you, you can shift. Tuhánee or not." Lily explained.

"I want to show you something. Can you come upstairs, Auntie Lily?" I asked.

Ethan helped Auntie Lily up, and we all went up into my room. Auntie Lily sat in the big leather chair by the window. Fancy Beast jumped into her lap. Lily pet Fancy Beast affectionately. The Beast purred, happily nuzzling Auntie Lily under her arm.

"Wow, she hates everyone but me." I was impressed.

"She knows who I am." Auntie Lily smiled. "Ah, I miss this room. Your grandmother used to stand out on the deck and paint. I would sit with her sometimes. She was so cool, my big sister." Lily looked out the window thoughtfully.

"Show her the ring." Jimmy interrupted.

I went into my nightstand and took the ring out.

"Do you know what this is?" I asked, showing Auntie Lily the gold lion ring.

Lily reached her hand out and I placed the ring in it. She turned it over and touched the relief of the mountain lion. She looked up at me, awestruck.

"Where did you get this?"

The book on my nightstand, *Pathways*, flew open and the pages fluttered in a wind that seemed to only be affecting the book. We all turned to the nightstand, as the book lay open to a page. Previously, the book was blank. Today however, there was an illustration of Frederick standing by the bookshelves, wearing the ring.

Ethan looked at it and we both exchanged the same look—shock.

I held the book for Auntie Lily to see. She took the book in hand and tilted her head looking at the image.

"This is my father, your great-grandfather, Frederick. You've seen him?" She looked at me knowingly.

"He gave me the ring in my vision." I took it from Auntie Lily and I showed her the inside, with the engraving of my name.

"He was buried with this ring on." Auntie Lily was quiet for a moment, thinking. "We are dangerously out of balance. The Earth, nature, the people. We are not in harmony. For so long now we have been ruining our world. Taking too much from the land. More than we need. We take the cutthroat trout from the lake, we take the silver and gold from the mountains. We take the trees from the forest. We take and we take and we take." Lily had tears in her eyes. "There is so little left, and yet we take more, giving so little back."

Lily stood up, looking out the window at the Lake. She turned and looked at the painting of the lake above my bed.

"Your Grandma Mae was afraid they would take the lake. So she painted it over and over so we would never forget it. And now it's still here, but it's not like it was. It's been changing. The lake is not as clear. The frackers are endangering it. It's suffered with all the pollution. The greed of the fishing. The litter. Our precious lake is changing. The magic of the water is getting tired. Our precious world is changing."

"Is the Watanuuk real, Auntie?" I asked, picking up the stuffed Watanuuk from the bed.

"They say when the birds fly away, the fish jump out of the lake dying, and the animals and weather behave strangely, then the Watanuuk is stirring below." Auntie Lily looked despondently out the window, staring at the lake. She held the ring out and handed it back to me.

"What can we do?" I asked, desperate.

"Wear this, always. You are doing what you can. Connecting and hearing the call of your animals. You'll feel more deeply. You'll adopt some of their traits. You will be the stewards of this Earth as you align yourselves with the animals. We must all change the way we live. Find ways to be kinder to our world; respect it and it will respect us. It is being demanded by nature. Because if it comes, we'll need to be powerful to defeat it. I'm afraid the fracking is awakening it, but you have been chosen. The ring is the confirmation that you hold the power."

"How do we defeat the Watanuuk?" I asked, terrified.

Auntie Lily was silent as she looked at the lake.

"Auntie?" I asked desperately.

"I've heard stories, but I'm not sure. There's a missing stone needed for a ritual. I wish I knew where it was." Her voice trembled as she turned and looked at the three of us, solemn. The house shook slightly. "The half moon is tonight. You must shift and quickly. I think we are running out of time."

"I'm calling a meeting. I'll get everyone together. My house in two hours." Ethan was on Discord, letting the pack know.

"I'll go get Felix." Jimmy looked concerned as he rushed out the door.

Ethan and I hustled down the stairs following Jimmy. Mom came in from the garage holding a big box.

"Whoa, where's the fire?" Mom laughed. Jimmy was out the door.

"Oh, we're going over to Ethan's, Mom. Auntie Lily is in my room. We gotta go."

"Wait, what is she doing in your room? How are you getting to Ethan's house? I have so many questions." Mom was amused.

I grabbed my snowboard and gear and was out the door.

"We're walking. I'm good," I yelled from the porch.

7

VOLCANO RUN

Ethan and I sat in his living room, waiting for everyone to arrive. I stoked the fire in the fireplace, warming my hands and watching the sapphire shine in the light. Luke was at work, and we were alone. Ethan sat close to me on the floor. I was scared to look at him. So much was happening; I was completely overwhelmed. As I thought about everything Auntie Lily said, I just stared into the flames, my eyes unfocused and my mind racing.

"Anya," Ethan said gently. "Anya?"

The emotions I was feeling were so big. I didn't know what to do with them all. I started to cry, my body filling up with too much water, too many thoughts, too many feelings. There wasn't enough room.

I started to sob and I felt embarrassed. Ethan immediately held onto me, hugging me so close. I could feel his heart beating through his sweatshirt. He smelled like honey and tangerines.

"I'm sorry," I choked out between tears.

"Sorry? For what?" Ethan looked at me with tears in his eyes. His kindness felt undeserved somehow.

"I cry too much. I always freak out. I'm so emotional." I sobbed.

"Look, this is some crazy, lunatic stuff. A creepy ancient lake monster might come out and destroy us. I think if there's a time to cry it's now. You're not overreacting. This is totally weird!" Ethan kinda laughed through his own tears.

"I guess I'm just used to feeling bad because my whole life I have been so impulsive and emotional. I'm always being told not to feel so much, or to stop overreacting. Now, I don't know what's appropriate. I never know what's appropriate." I sighed, sniffing.

"Anya, we're *all* this way. All of us. Jimmy. Felix, Me, Lily, Iris, Faye and Lucy. Are you kidding me? We are all *like this*. I get angry over noth-ing, all the time. I'm a complete spaz. Faye breaks stuff. We feel things in ways other "normal" people don't," Ethan made big hand quotes and rolled his eyes.

"Really?" It felt unbelievable that I wasn't alone.

"Yes, really! Why do you think the animals are connecting to us? Because we can hear them. We are listening. Anya, we have senses most people don't have, think about it. That's why we get over-whelmed. This world is designed for people who aren't paying atten-tion. They have filters. We take it all in. And I think, more and more kids are like us. Like the new generation. They call us neurodiverse. Whatever. Different. Problematic. Overly sensitive. Difficult. Weird. Right?" Ethan was looking directly at me.

"Yeah, I've heard all that. My dad never has understood me. My mom does, but my dad has no patience and now he's gone and it's my fault," I cried, letting out my biggest fear.

"He didn't leave because of you. He left because he couldn't deal with *his* life and the decisions *he* made. That's his loss. My mom left us. She couldn't handle me. I was so hard as a little kid. I had terrible tantrums. I broke things, I threw stuff, I screamed. I was possessed. I didn't speak until I was almost five. She didn't know what to do with me. I wasn't what she signed up for. My dad, he is everything I could want and more. He always knows how to talk to me. Sometimes I get sad about my mom, but mostly I just feel bad for her now. Think of all she is missing out on." Ethan jumped up and made a grand gesture at himself spinning around in circles. "All this! Her loss."

Our tears turned to laughter as Ethan extended his hand and helped me stand up.

"We just gotta dance the fear away."

Ethan ran over to Luke's record player. He put on a song I had never heard before. *Doctor, My Eyes* played by Jackson Browne.

"My dad and his 70's obsession, but this is a good one." Ethan laughed holding my hands and dancing with me. It was so corny, but the song washed away my anxiety and we smiled and laughed as I wiped the tears from my eyes. "Redirection baby. It always works." Ethan laughed.

"It sure does." The doorbell rang. The pack was here. We had business to discuss.

Everyone filed in and sat around the living room.

Jimmy stood up. "OK, I filled everyone in for the most part, on the drive over."

"Wait, you drive?" I asked Jimmy. I couldn't imagine him driving, he seemed so young.

"I drive. I got my license last month." Felix said sticking his hand up. "Influencer money—got a Lexus SUV." Felix stood up and took a bow.

"Flex, honey, flex." Jimmy laughed.

"Dang." I was impressed.

Ethan stood up. "OK. Tonight is the night. It's the half moon, and we need to connect as a pack. I think Anya has been the missing piece all this time. According to Auntie Lily we might be able to shape-shift now that we are all together."

"We each need to call our animal spirit. Ask them to come out. Like I did with the bears." Faye stated.

"Yeah, but how exactly do you do that? What if I don't do it right?" I was worried. "Is it that simple?"

"It's going to work. You just visualize, and ask in your mind." Terra was confident.

"Tonight, the clearing." Lucy stated.

"But first... we gotta take advantage of all this fresh powder!" Ethan was running back and forth across the couch and launched off, kicking his feet out behind him.

"I am so supportive of this idea." Iris stood up, her tail swaying side to side, as she jumped up and down matching Ethan's energy.

"YES!" Felix was up and jumping. The whole pack got on their feet, ready to snowboard. "I'll drive. Obviously." Felix stated.

"You all just have to endure his '80s playlist. It's all he listens to." Jimmy teased.

"As long as we can hear "Danger Zone," I'm fine with it." Terra added.

"It's fourth on the playlist!" Felix did some ridiculous dance called the Carlton. I didn't know what that meant, but it was fantastically nerdy.

We headed to North Veil Summit as "Space Junk" by Devo was playing, the roads crunchy under the snow tires. My mind was on fire thinking about how much my life had changed in the last month. I watched the snowy terrain fly by the car window. Everyone was chattering, the car buzzing with conversations. I was quiet; I thought about Robin, who I hadn't talked to in over a week. She'd reached out to me, but I didn't even know how to explain my life. Then I thought about my dad. He had sent me a letter, but it was still unopened on my desk. Maybe I'll never open it. All this made me sad, yet I was so full of excitement being a part of this pack, knowing Ethan, learning about my heritage and just the wild idea I may shift into a frickin' mountain lion tonight. It seemed completely insane. How would anyone explain it?

"Are you OK?" Ethan saw I was far away.

I smiled at him warmly. "I'm actually great. Just in my busy head."

"I know all about that." Ethan smiled back broadly. "We should be at North Veil soon. It's got great runs."

"I'm rusty. I may be on my butt a lot." I laughed.

"I'm always on my butt, we can be bad at this together." Lucy laughed.

"You'll be fine." Ethan assured me.

Once there I looked up at the beauty. It was breathtaking. Mammoth had nothing on this.

"OK we're going on the Shiver blade Drop run." Felix led the way.

"Anya, did you know we're snowboarding on a volcano?" Iris informed me.

"No." I was intrigued.

"Mt. Black. Don't worry, it hasn't erupted for 2 million years." Iris reassured me.

"Hopefully it doesn't wake up, I feel like things are waking up." Jimmy winced.

"Jimmy don't jinx this. It's a good day!" Ethan barked.

Everyone had their gear on. Ethan helped adjust my goggles. We rode to the top of the mountain on the gondola. The views were crazy beautiful. I felt that elated sensation I got when I was with the mountain lions. My whole body was electric. Terra, Jimmy and Iris all had tails affixed to their snow suits. They looked so cute. The mountain was remarkably quiet. Even though it was a heavy snow day, not many people were out, which seemed strange to me. How could you not want to be here like, every minute of every day?

We all started down the mountain, cutting back and forth. It was a steep run, not for beginners. But I felt oddly agile in a way I never felt before. Everyone was flying down the run with such grace and expertise. It was spectacular. Ethan was in front of me, and pointed to the trees to the right. I looked over and saw a mountain lion running down the hill, keeping pace with me. I laughed out loud, amazed. The lion was cutting around the trees and playfully keeping up with me. He disappeared into the forest. I headed towards him and although logically I felt that was a super stupid thing to do, I also knew I had to follow him. Ethan was close behind me on his board. He was always watching out for me. We went off-piste in search of my lion. We whipped through some trees and followed the lion's footprints in the fresh snow. I stopped and looked around. Ethan came to an elegant stop behind me.

"Did we lose him?" He asked, breathless. I removed the goggles from my eyes, hoping to get a clearer look.

"I think so." I breathed heavily.

Just as I said that, the lion walked out from behind a fallen tree. He leaped on to the top of the trunk and stared at us. My heart was all I could hear. He jumped down from the huge fallen tree and landed directly in front of me, landing with a heavy thud. Ethan breathed in sharply.

The mountain lion edged closer to me, carefully eyeing me with his nostrils flaring. I slowly took my glove off, my lion ring glistening in the light. I put my hand out the way you offer your hand to a house cat or a small dog you're trying to befriend. This was entirely different and probably insane, but it's what I did.

The mountain lion let out a rumbling noise that I could feel in my chest. It sounded like a purr, but deeper. I stood very still, with my hand extended. I was shaking slightly, but overall relatively calm under the circumstances.

The lion lunged forward a little bit and pushed his head up into my palm, requesting pets. I carefully and gently obliged. He started to purr for real, and though it was soothing the purrs rumbled all the way up my arm, vibrating like the engine of some giant machine. As I touched his head, the sapphire ring on my finger glowed. My entire body vibrated the exact same way I felt in my visions, with the statues. Ethan was silent and standing very still behind me, watching. I could hear him breathing. The mountain lion looked directly into my eyes, and then turned and ran into the thickness of the forest.

I whipped around and looked at Ethan, his face frozen in a permanent smile.

"That was AMAZING!" He shrieked. We both instantly hugged one another, cackling with delight. Mostly because we didn't die, but also because we could tell the connection was real.

We put our gear back on and started boarding back out onto the run. The rest of the pack was nowhere in sight. Ethan and I continued side by side down the mountain. A sudden shadow swept over us. I looked up — it was Ethan's eagle. As I was about to alert him, I saw he was already watching it, arms stretched out like he was flying down the slope. As we snowboarded down the hill, the eagle swooped lower and hovered right over Ethan. He landed directly on his right arm, almost knocking him over. But the bird flapped his massive wings and pulled him almost off the ground to steady him. I was next to them and could feel the wind generated from the mighty flapping. Ethan and his eagle descended down the run together.

A jump was coming up to the right, and I could sense Ethan thinking he wanted to attempt it with his winged pal. Both of them veered towards the jump. I peeled off to the right, slowing to a stop to watch. I wasn't the only one. Several snowboarders and skiers were stopped, standing slack-jawed at this incredible moment. Ethan launched off the jump, and his eagle dug into his snow suit with his talons, holding tight. As the two flew off the jump the eagle flapped his wings with great effort. The two went off the jump beautifully, and held air for what seemed like hundreds of feet. Ethan was whoo-hoo-ing with joy as the eagle gently and skillfully landed Ethan on the ground, where he continued snowboarding down the course effortlessly. It was delightful. The eagle let go of Ethan, and flew to the trees above, landing to keep watch. A group of skiers cheered and screamed in total disbelief, throwing their ski poles and hats into the air. I hopped back on my board and raced down the run to catch up with Ethan. The other pack members were already most likely at the bottom of the run. I caught up to Ethan, whose face was flushed red with excitement.

"I WAS FLYING!!" he screamed.

I stood, my mouth wide open, no words available. Finally, jumping up and down, I blurted out, "AAAHHHHH!!!" We embraced quickly, then parted to gape in amazement again. "AAAAHHHH," we yelled.

Giddy, we continued down the run. I was snowboarding better than I ever had in my life. Ethan and I were in total unison all the way to the bottom. Absolute euphoria.

The rest of the pack were waiting on us by the gondola. "Hey, where did you guys go? You missed the coolest thing!" Terra exclaimed.

Ethan and I looked at one another and started laughing.

"What?" Terra was now laughing too, but they had no idea why.

"Wait, what happened to you?" I asked.

"A wolf showed up and ran out in front of me on the run. It was so huge. It ran right by me and then with me for a few minutes." Terra was glowing.

"It was insane." Jimmy had somehow found hot chocolate.

"What happened to you two?" Felix asked, also drinking hot chocolate. I was feeling jealous about all the chocolate.

"Well, Anya met her mountain lion." Ethan beamed.

"WHAT, no! More words now!" Iris demanded.

"I saw him way up the mountain before the jumps. He was running along side of me and then we went off-piste into the trees where he disappeared." I was breathing hard even thinking about it.

"Yeah, but we thought we lost him, and then he came out and walked *right up to Anya*. She petted him. It was so wild." Ethan was almost hyperventilating.

"Well, and then Ethan flew with an eagle off a jump." I added, nonchalantly. "Or the eagle flew Ethan off the jump is more like it." I giggled.

"WHAT!?" Lucy and Faye said in unison. The rest of the pack looked dizzy with delight.

Jimmy took his hot cocoa and threw it into the trash can dramatically. "That's it, we need to get back up there. I have raccoons to bond with." Jimmy marched towards the gondolas.

"If a bear doesn't build a snowman with me, I'm out of here." Faye said, deadpan. We almost fell over laughing.

We rode up the gondolas to the top of the mountain. I was still vibrating from the adrenaline. Ethan held my hand on the way up.

"Can you feel it?" He said.

I felt like I was going to throw up. I wasn't sure what he was referring to.

I just looked at him, shifting my eyes around nervously.

"This is pure frickin' magic, Anya. This volcano we're riding on, this land is all a part of us. And I'm feeling myself intertwined with all this... beauty." Ethan had tears in his eyes.

I squeezed his hand tightly. "This is like nothing I could have imagined." I smiled, losing myself in his blue eyes.

The second run down the mountain proved to be as mind-blowing as the first. This time Ethan and I hung back as Felix rode the mountain with two deer by his side. They bounced through the snow like they were on springs, Jimmy behind him with a raccoon racing him down the run.

We stopped part way down the mountain as we saw Faye off to the side in the trees, sitting next to a large black bear who was resting her head in Faye's lap.

We hopped back on our boards and crisscrossed down the mountain. Ahead, I saw Lucy waving at us to stop. She looked to be in distress. We cut over to the left near a thick forest of trees.

I pushed my goggles up over my helmet. "What's wrong, Lucy?"

"It's Iris, we were snowboarding off the run and she got stuck in the snow. A pile of snow fell on top of her and I can't get her free! I don't know if she can breathe; it's a lot of snow!" Lucy was freaking out.

Ethan and I followed Lucy through the trees and rushed to get to Iris. Lucy pointed ahead by some boulders where the snow had fallen from. "She's under there." Lucy panted. As we approached, I saw snow shooting up in the air, like someone had turned on a snow blower.

"Iris!!" Ethan called out.

We all got closer, and what we saw was like something out of a cartoon. Three foxes were all digging Iris out of the snow, their back feet kicking out the snow surrounding Iris in a jet, their tails wiggling madly. At the bottom of the hole, we saw her glove, then her face poking out.

"I'm OK." She panted. "They've been digging me out." All three foxes were surrounding Iris, working feverishly to get her unburied. Ethan used his board to try and help free Iris more. As Iris got dug clear, I reached down to help her up. As she popped out of the hole in the snow, Lucy backed out to give her room and then gave a yelp.

"Guys look!" Lucy yelled. "They all came out." One squirrel was on her head and two on her shoulders.

We all laughed, even Iris, who was relieved but obviously still a little shaken.

"What happened?" Ethan asked, concerned.

"I swerved to miss what I thought was a squirrel and crashed into the tree, not that hard, but it set off a mini-avalanche above on the boulders and a bunch of snow piled on top of me. I got buried. I couldn't move at all. The more I tried to move and couldn't, the more panicked I became. I heard Lucy yelling, and then before I knew it I saw my foxes digging me out." Iris was petting one of the foxes who was making cute purring noises. The other two foxes were running and playing around the trees. Lucy's squirrels ran down her body and began playing with the foxes.

We all stood around, watching the squirrels and foxes play. Then, Iris said goodbye to her fox heroes. The four of us got clipped back into our boards and headed out to the run. It was getting late and we needed to get going. At the bottom of the run we all met up and just looked at one another, speechless for a minute, and for Ethan, that was saying something.

All at once, the laughter exploded out of us.

"Let's get back, we have a long evening ahead of us." Felix advised.

No one could shut up in the car on the way back to Ethan's. "Did you see the bear? He was literally rolling down the run and then just relaxed next to me with his head in my lap!" Faye was beside herself.

"That was pure madness. I mean all these animals. The food chain. Nobody was eating one another." I was shocked.

"I think this connection transcends the predatory instinct. We are here to connect for a bigger purpose." Jimmy said thoughtfully.

"Your mountain lion was so incredible," Ethan marveled.

"Right? He was gorgeous." I felt delirious. We pulled into the driveway behind Luke's Bronco. Everyone piled out of Felix's SUV, laughing and talking a mile a minute. The excitement was palpable. We threw our boards around the front porch and went inside to warm up and grab snacks. We had a lot to prepare for.

8

NEW SKIN

Inside we peeled off our snow gear. The fire was already burning, and Luke came downstairs. "Hey, how was the snow?" He asked.

"Dad, it was the best run we have ever had. The snow was perfect and we tore it up." Ethan was extra hyper.

"You guys want some dinner?" Luke asked.

"No, we're gonna just grab some snacks and head out," Ethan said.

"Where are you off to? You just got back," Luke asked.

"We're going to the clearing," Iris said.

Ethan was already packing bags with firewood, cookies and kindling. He was also collecting as many flashlights as he could find. "I have about three flashlights but with the snow and the half moon there should be plenty of light. Here's some snacks guys." Ethan threw out chips, cookies and protein bars at everyone.

"Don't be too late. Tomorrow is a school day." Luke pointed a finger at Ethan.

"Yes Dad. Whatever you say Dad," Ethan said in his best robot voice.

The walk to the clearing was filled with nervous energy. The pack was excited, unsure what to expect. We didn't talk much. The night sky was remarkably clear, and the stars were on display. The moon lit our path; we didn't even need the flashlights. I could smell distant fireplace smells and pine. It was glorious. Ethan led the way, my boots crunching snow in a satisfying way. The clearing was quiet, and the moon bounced off the snow, illuminating everything with a beautiful glow.

Ethan got to work on building a fire. It was cold. The girls ran around the clearing doing their quadrobics to warm up. I watched with admiration at their skill level and how fast they could go. They chased each other, fell over, chased each other some more, and laughed. The fire was underway, and I watched Felix and Jimmy sitting together under the moonlight. Terra was helping Ethan with the fire and I just stared at the moon. It was so pretty in the sky. I was exactly where I belonged.

"OK everyone, the fire is ready. Come warm up," Terra announced, their voice echoing through the clearing.

Everyone settled around the fire, warming their hands.

"Anya, we have been out here so many times trying to fully connect with our theriotypes, but we think you have been what we were missing. I'm so grateful for your friendship, your presence, and whatever happens tonight, I am so glad you're here with us as part of our pack." Faye announced. The pack all agreed in nods and thumbs up.

"100% Faye. 100%." Lucy chimed in.

Jimmy stood up, removing a small drum from his backpack. "There's a chant I am going to lead you in while I play the drum. Join in when you feel ready. Everyone else hold hands, I will remain inside the circle leading the chant. As we chant, visualize your theriotype and as you do, see yourself as one with them. Ask them to come to the clearing and assist with the connection. Thank them for coming. Anyone have questions?" Jimmy's face was wild with excitement.

"I mean I think I have about a hundred questions. But, what then? Like, will we know how to shift back to human form or something? Will my clothes fly off me like the Hulk? How does it all work Jimmy? I don't want to be nude out here in the snow." I asked needing all the info.

Jimmy looked around at everyone, holding his Tuhánee drum, his raccoon makeup sparkling in the firelight. "I have no flipping idea Anya. I think we just see what happens." Jimmy started giggling, and his nervous laughter caught on.

"Look, we will be OK. We feel it, don't we, that we are somehow protected? Like we felt today on the slopes. I felt electrified in a way I've never felt before. We did moves none of us have the skill level to do. The animals were with us, giving us their agility. You all felt it, right?" Ethan asked with a knowing expression.

"Yeah, I definitely never snowboarded like that before." I said.

Terra added, "That was next level for sure."

"I'm usually crying ten minutes into snowboarding and landing on my butt so many times I rage quit. Not today. That was epic." Lucy laughed.

"I mean, I crashed, but the foxes got me out." Iris laughed.

"See, we don't have to be afraid. We're protected." Jimmy said confidently. "I might not know how this is all going down, but I am sure we are meant to do this. Auntie Lily wouldn't steer us wrong. Now join hands."

The pack all joined hands. The fire crackled and popped. A cold breeze whipped around the clearing, creating tiny snow tornados.

Everyone was quiet. I visualized my mountain lions. I called them to the clearing in my mind and thanked them for coming. I could see them in the moonlit path in my mind as they walked side by side.

Jimmy began beating the drum rhythmically, slowly at first, but finding his beat. The sound of the drum was hypnotizing. I could feel the hands of Terra and Ethan on either side of me, holding me tightly. In my mind I watched the lions walking side by side, swaying in unison with one another. Everyone's eyes were closed as the drumbeat continued.

Jimmy began the Tuhánee chant. It was discordant and odd, but it built momentum, and soon revealed a circular chant that repeated over and over. Some of the pack joined in as they caught on. I waited, listening, and feeling the power of the chant. Almost like the pause before you enter a double dutch jump rope. It pulsed through me in a very powerful way. As I caught the wave of the chant, I joined in, and now everyone in the pack was chanting together. The drum thumped against my heart. It became automatic and filled the clearing with a beautiful sound.

What we didn't notice as we chanted and visualized was that the clearing was surrounded by our animals. They all entered the clearing slowly and gathered around us. Faye and her black bear were lined up. Ethan's bald eagle was perched behind him on a nearby tree. My two mountain lions lay behind me in the snow. A family of squirrels and raccoons were scattered around the circle. Felix's deer, a doe and a buck, entered the clearing, walking slowly towards the fire. A small fox walked next to a wolf, coexisting peacefully as the chanting brought everyone together.

We were all so focused in this hypnotic state that no one opened their eyes. Anyone seeing this from above would have been flabbergasted: a clearing filled with every wild animal from the Emerald area. Even animals none of us connected to showed up. Bats flew around erratically as a bobcat walked across the clearing. A pack of coyotes looked on from the forest. Skunks chattered, running around playfully, and I could see owls in the trees.

The chanting continued, and I could no longer feel Ethan or Terra's hands. I felt nothing, yet everything; my body pulsed with tremendous energy. The chant continued, and the animals kept arriving: more bears, more foxes, more raccoons. The clearing was thronged with wildlife.

I started to feel a similar feeling to when I connect to my astral dreams. There was an electrical buzzing and a feeling of floating. I kept visualizing my lions, and pictured them next to me, my body and theirs merging. The chanting became farther away as I felt myself lift out of my body. I could see the clearing from above, a massive congregation of animals, and us in the middle around a fire, holding hands. There was only a split second where I felt as if I were floating, and then with a profound racing feeling, my vision changed completely.

I was running faster than I ever had, my heartbeat pounding like a war drum in my ears. My muscles felt strange—longer, coiled with power—and my paws (paws?) tore over the snow in a blur. I turned my head to the right and a bear thundered beside me. The night lit up as though someone had flipped a giant switch; between the half moon and the snow, it was almost like daylight. My vision stretched wide, catching every flicker of movement in huge, crystal-clear vistas. Most strangely, I *knew* exactly where I was in the landscape, as if some new, ancient map had been etched inside me.I ran up the mountain, jetting between trees and over boulders with tremendous speed and agility. I was running with three other mountain lions, and I could understand them. They wanted to show me a place at the top of the mountain, overlooking everything.

As I followed them, I was filled with an almost unbelievable feeling of freedom and exhilaration, and I could also hear everyone else from the pack. Not so much talking—more like a knowing, that everyone had shifted and were exploring the Sierras with their theriotypes. It was such a pure harmony and a connection that, although we were having our own explorations, we could also tap into each other and feel the collective experience. It was like being omnipresent, and at this moment I knew everything and everyone was one. The messy debris of people's petty disagreements and cynical views about stupid stuff suddenly lost all importance; I knew we really were all connected. How did we get so far away from one another?

The lions led the way, and I jumped and danced from rock to rock, over fallen trees and up steep inclines. And then, after an almost effortless experience of climbing the Sierras, we were perched on a high ledge, thousands of feet above the lake. The half moon reflected off the water, sparkling with the gift of the glowing light. I could feel my animal's heart beating, the blood flowing through my body.

The views and the towering pines underneath me gave me a feeling of invincibility, but at the same time, a sense of how small I really was in the giant picture. We all stretched out on the flat rock, taking in the beauty of the Lake.

As we rested, I began to feel the weird new senses I had acquired more intensely. Smells were not only more intense, but told a story; I could smell the different soils and plants we had tracked through on our way up, and I could page through them like a book, sensing each part of our journey in order. I could identify each of my lion companions by scent, as clearly as my human form could tell the difference between a pineapple and a Christmas tree. In a separate new sense, I somehow knew exactly where I was, as though I had some sort of GPS inside my head.

In the distance I noticed a clearing in the trees, where I could see lights, odd buildings, and cranes. As I looked, my GPS—I couldn't think of anything better to call it—felt glitchy and off at the area of the clearing. I glanced at the lions, and we knew. The frackers. The cold wind ruffled through my fur, a feeling so foreign, yet pleasing.

The cliff shelf we were on shook with a jolt, and within minutes the sky was full of hawks: hundreds of them, flapping madly, agitated. I could see a disturbance in the lake, what looked like little whitecaps in the water. I realized it was the fish jumping out of the water, the way they did when we were on the pier. Something was terribly wrong.

The mountain lions stood up and stretched, I joined them and felt flexible and light. They jumped off the ledge and onto the side of the mountain, making their way down. We all ran together, back the way we came through the woods, at lightning speed.

The snow began to fall. I felt the pack communicating with me to meet at Ethan's house. The mountain lion companions understood where I needed to go and took me through the woods and towards the house. We were so quick and nimble. A freak storm had come out of nowhere—the snow blew almost sideways, and I could hear, in the distance, the crackle and thud of a tree falling. What had started as a beautiful snowfall was turning into a real problem. We dodged falling branches and as I ran, I could feel the temperature dropping quickly.

I saw Ethan's house in the distance as we made our way down the mountain; above the house I saw Ethan in his eagle form, flying circles around the house, almost like a beacon. I kept running towards him, focused on escaping the chaos of the forest. My lion companions wanted to leave for the shelter of their dens; my new senses made this clear to me in ways I didn't understand but were as clear as speech. We stopped maybe a hundred feet from Ethan's. I thanked them for their help, and I turned around and watched them run back up the hill. I felt so much love.

I could see police lights flashing in the driveway of Ethan's place. The pack was all returning to the backyard—we all connected mentally. I started to run the rest of the way to the house when I realized I was back in my human body. It happened almost without my knowledge. The transition from animal to human was seamless and luckily all of my clothes were intact!

The wind was almost unbearable without my dense lion fur. I ran to the big A-frame home, dodging branches and the stinging wind. In spite of the mind-bending evening, I felt calm. I wasn't overwhelmed. I felt peaceful and exactly right. Mom's car was in the driveway with several cars I didn't recognize, along with a cop car.

9

BUSTED

The pack met behind Ethan's house in the trees a few yards from the back door. Everyone was back in their bodies. We just stood looking at one another in total, euphoric disbelief while the storm raged around us. We didn't even take a minute to talk about all that happened; we had to get out of the storm, and fast.

"What, it's 2 a.m.?!" Ethan blurted out. "We lost track of time!"

"There's cops here." I said.

"I'm sure everyone is going crazy looking for us. What do we say?" Terra was panicked.

"I'll do the talking," Ethan said. "Just follow my lead."

We ran to the back door and piled into the warm house. The kitchen was empty, but I could hear parents gathered in the living room, speaking in hushed tones.

Mom ran into the kitchen when she heard the door open.

"Anya!" She ran over to me, hugging me tightly. I hugged her back and I could feel her shaking. God, I scared the hell out of her.

"We're OK Mom, we're OK."

We all walked into the living room together, where a crowd of parents and a policeman, Officer Brett, all swiveled their heads with a look of shock and relief.

"Felix!" his mom jumped up and ran to hug him. Iris's dad made his way to Iris and grabbed her, hugging her tightly. Iris wasn't a hugger, so she went all stiff and looked horribly uncomfortable. Her dad didn't care; he couldn't let go.

Officer Brett shook his head, aggravated. "Kids, it's dangerous out there. We thought you'd be found dead in this storm. I had crews out there looking for you, but I had to call them off; the storm was too bad. The clearing was empty. Where were you?"

Auntie Lily was sitting next to the fireplace calmly. She looked at me and we locked eyes. I nodded slightly. She cracked a smile, proud.

"We were out in the clearing, having a bonfire. Everything seemed fine." Ethan started explaining. "Then the temperature dropped super fast and the wind started going crazy. We decided it would be safer if we took shelter and waited for the storm to blow over."

"Took shelter where?" Mom asked completely confused.

"There is nothing out there." Officer Brett barked.

Auntie Lily stepped in. "I know there is that cave near the clearing. Did you all hide in there?" She asked prompting us.

"Yes, the one to the north? We built a little fire inside the cave and stayed there. No one had any cell service, I guess with the storm. And the cave. So we stayed there for a long time, waiting the storm out." Ethan stammered.

Felix's mom chimed in. "But it's worse now than it was, how the heck did you all get back here? You all look dry and fine? It doesn't make any sense."

"Yea, we noticed a lull in the storm and decided to just run back as fast as we could. Luckily, we were fine, and when we got back here the storm seemed to pick up again." Jimmy said, convincingly.

"OK, everyone who has parents here get home. The others, Jimmy, Faye, Lucy and Terra, I am dropping you off. Your parents are home and terrified. Call them and let them know you're OK and that we're on the way. Let's get going. I should be in bed with my dog," Officer Brett sighed with exasperation.

Auntie Lily stood up and walked over to me, holding my hand, smiling. Mom looked confused and rattled, to say the least. Luke was hugging Ethan, relieved.

"Thank you Brett. I'm so sorry." Luke said.

"Yeah, yeah.." Brett was shuffling the kids out the door. "I don't know why you kids hang out in that clearing. It's too remote. Stay closer to home next time."

Everyone looked at each other, a little stunned and amused, as they left the house.

Mom walked over to Luke. They exchanged a sweet, relieved glance. Luke hugged Mom warmly.

"They're OK." he assured her. "I knew they would be OK."

Mom smiled and rubbed Luke's arm.

"Thank you." She glowed a little, looking at him.

Ethan walked over to me. He looked into my eyes and made huge, wide, excited eyes at me. Forcing himself to remain cool. Then he did a *mind blown* gesture with his hands. I nodded quietly in agreement.

"Ethan, thanks for keeping us safe and calm out there. I didn't know storms happened so quickly like that." I said, setting him up as the hero.

"They don't, Anya. This was a real freak occurrence." Luke looked worried. "Do you guys want to stay here tonight? I can rustle up blankets and we have the extra bedrooms."

"No, Luke, we just want to get home. It's not too far and I have the 4 wheel drive. But thank you." Mom smiled as she helped Auntie Lily out the door. I followed, Felix and his mom behind us, and Iris and her dad behind them. Luke stood at the door, watching us get into the car.

The car ride home was strange. I could feel Mom wanting to talk to me but also completely NOT wanting to talk to me. She was white-knuckling the drive home as the wind unsteadied the car. Auntie Lily sat in the front seat humming, which was annoying Mom. I was in the backseat, lost in thought about the insane evening I'd just had.

"Auntie Lily, you're spending the night, right?" I asked. "You shouldn't drive home in this weather."

"Yes Auntie, you are staying with us." Mom was adamant. "I don't know how these roads are going to look tomorrow. Obviously schools will be closed, and I have no idea if we'll be snowed in or what."

"Yes, I'll stay. I look forward to chatting more with Anya tomorrow." Auntie Lily turned around and smiled at me.

Mom was distracted and worried. Even though I was safe, I could sense her fears. Wait, I could sense her fears? I sat in the backseat realizing I had new abilities. There was a smell coming off of Mom that I registered as fear. I wondered: what other abilities had I gained?

We pulled into the driveway; I was completely awake, even though it was after three o'clock. The adrenaline rush from the night was going to make it impossible to sleep. I helped Auntie Lily out of the car and walked her up the stairs to the front door of the cabin. The storm was raging. As Mom was rushing to get the keys out to get us inside, the screen door flew open and almost off the hinges. Mom got the door open and we all piled inside, trying to escape the brutally cold wind.

The fire was still lit, but was pitiful. Auntie Lily sat on the couch and I worked on getting the fire going again. The house was warm from the heater, but I was afraid we would lose power.

"Good idea, we may not have power much longer," Mom said.

"I'll get it going." I added newspaper and kindling. The fire began to grow.

"Does anyone want any tea or hot cocoa?" Mom was so domestic. It's how she deals with stress.

"Yes. I would like that mint tea, thank you, Mary," Auntie said.

"I'll take some of that too, with some honey."

Mom wandered into the kitchen to make our tea. The wind was so loud around the cabin and through the trees. Fancy Beast trotted down the stairs and jumped on the couch with Auntie.

"You shifted tonight?" Auntie Lily whispered, delighted.

"We did, Auntie. All of us. It was incredible. I feel different," I whispered as I poked the fire.

"I never shifted; I didn't have the pack to connect to in order to transform. This isn't typical. Frederick, my father, he shifted. He told me stories when I was little. You are all meant for something special. There's a reason you shift. Listen to your animals. Listen to the land, and you will feel what your purpose is with all this new ability." Auntie Lily stroked Fancy Beast, who was on her back demanding pets.

Mom came into the living room, holding a tray with tea and some cookies. She looked tired.

"Here, this should warm you both up." Mom placed the tray on the coffee table.

"Thanks Mom. I'm going to drink this in bed and get some sleep. I'm so tired." I wasn't, I really just wanted to avoid Mom, as I knew she was uneasy about the night and I wasn't quite ready for any pointed questions.

"Good night Anya." Auntie Lily smiled.

"I'm glad you're OK, honey." Mom sighed and sat in front of the fire with her tea. I hugged her goodnight, and headed upstairs.

I bathed, warming my bones, reflecting on the night. Afterwards, wrapped in my favorite robe, I watched the storm from the window. It raged so violently that the lights flickered, threatening to cut power. I could feel the restlessness of the animals.

I got into bed, still wide awake, and picked up the book on the night-stand. It was open to the drawing of Frederick wearing the ring. I paged through the book, expecting to see the blank pages, but instead it was filled with page after page of drawings.

Every page was telling a story. It started at the beginning when the coyote led the Tuhánee to the lake. The beauty of the land, and the harmony that followed the arrival of the Tuhánee. Their pine-nut harvesting and festivals. Beautiful basket weaving. The hand games they played. Joyous times.

But the stories became dark as the changes came that shifted nature out of balance. It showed the gold and silver rush, and all the destruction the mining created. The greed, and the horrors the Tuhánee faced from terrible mistreatment. Illustrations of Cave Rock and the Eshooni, Shamans meditating, animals and shapeshifting. And the Watanuuk.

There were no words, but you could follow the history through the drawings. Pages of The Watanuuk ripping out of the lake and destroying homes, land, killing people, sowing chaos. My heart raced as I saw the entire history of Emerald; I felt it deep in my soul and knew this was a warning. The last time the Watanuuk came was many years ago, during the most recent disregard for the sacredness of Cave Rock. It showed climbers drilling spikes in the rock, and clambering all over, their ropes tangled across the face of it. The Eshooni were depicted as vague shapes, but I could tell they were fierce with anger. It showed a woman painting the lake on the shore. It was Grandma Mae from the photograph, the one taken by a young Auntie Lily. More pages revealed a gathering and meditation with the Tuhánee elders. One page showed a piece of jewelry, a necklace pouch made of what looked like leather and beads. Inside was a carved stone with an eagle. The drawings made clear this stone was sacred. It was shown throughout the book, and was obviously significant.

Somehow the Watanuuk was lured back to his nest by one of the Tuhánee, who was holding the eagle stone. A seal was placed around the nest, keeping the Watanuuk below. I shut the book and tucked it under my pillow, sighing. My phone dinged and I looked at the message.

Are you OK? I miss you.

I realized I had ignored the last several messages Robin left me, and that she was up in the middle of the night, worried! I texted back.

I'm so sorry I've been AFK. It's been a weird week. I'll catch you up tomorrow. I promise.

K.

I lay in bed trying to fall asleep, but it felt impossible. It had been such a wild night. The storm was still intense outside, but despite the noise of the wind Fancy Beast was sound asleep on the chair. On my nightstand was a candle I had found in my closet boxes. It was a candle Robin had bought me that smelled like pine trees. Her joke, knowing I was moving to Emerald where everything smelled like pine trees. I smiled as I lit it. The room glowed as the candle flickered and light danced on the ceiling. It was soothing and I closed my eyes, thinking of Ethan. As I started to drift off, I heard Fancy Beast make a low guttural sound. My eyes shot open and I saw what was freaking her out. On the deck rail perched a giant bald eagle staring into my bedroom window. I hopped out of bed and went to the deck door to open it. As I opened the door Ethan stood outside, smiling. "Can I come inside." He whispered.

"That was you! You shifted again?" I was amazed, letting him inside and throwing the blanket from the chair around him to warm him up.

"Yea, we can shift on our own now. We just needed to do it the first time together, I guess?" Ethan shrugged, amused and delighted.

"Oh wow. This is incredible," I laughed, trying not to make any loud noises.

"I couldn't sleep, so I went outside and before I knew it I was flying over the lake. The storm is still pretty bad, but somehow I did just fine navigating it in eagle form, so I flew here to see you." Ethan smiled sheepishly. "Is that OK?"

"Yes. I want to show you something." I sat on my bed and got the book out from under my pillow. "Look at this."

Ethan sat next to me on my bed; my heart was beating so fast I could feel it in my throat. He was wrapped in the blanket and looked so handsome. He took the book, looking at all the drawings.

"It's everything." He looked at me, stunned.

"Well, it's definitely the history. But I'm not sure exactly what it all means for what's happening now. Look, see these pages with the necklace. I think this is significant." I pointed to the necklace with the eagle stone.

Ethan flipped back through the drawings, looking at everything, studying the meaning. "So I think they did some sort of ritual to put the Watanuuk back into the nest. Like a seal? See here where it comes out of the Lake, and all the craziness." Ethan was pointing to the Watanuuk's destruction around Cave Rock, and in earlier drawings around the gold rush. "I think it comes out when things get way out of whack and it avenges everyone. When people ignore taking care of nature. But it looks like there's a lot of collateral damage in the process." The images show the Watanuuk with people in its talons, death everywhere, homes and buildings being crushed by its massive wings. Total chaos.

"I mean if it was this insane, why isn't everyone talking about it all the time. Like Bigfoot or something." I was confused.

"I don't know. I know the Tuhánee have been very vocal about the legends, always, but maybe since everything needs to be seen to be believed these days, word-of-mouth doesn't mean much anymore. Think about it. Even if there was video of the Watanuuk going ape-crap bananas, would anyone believe it? Oh it's AI, they'd say, or it's fake. We're in such a weird place now, where truth isn't truth anymore," Ethan sighed sadly.

"Ape crap bananas?" I giggled.

"I'm trying to stop swearing." Ethan chuckled. "Is that a good one?"

"Very. Anyways, I think we have to get prepared. We have to figure out how to fix it all. I mean if the Watanuuk does come out, it could be disastrous." I said as I slipped under the covers, chilly.

Ethan climbed into the bed with me, almost instinctively, pulling the covers up to his chin, warming up.

"Do you feel different? Since the shift." He asked.

I did. But underneath the warmth of the blanket and the thrill of being this close, there was an undercurrent, like the lake itself was holding its breath. The Watanuuk wasn't just a story anymore—it was a clock ticking.

"I do." I turned my head sideways on the pillow, looking right at him. "Do you?"

"I can feel so much more. I can sense people's feelings. I can see so much better. My eyes are sharp. And my hearing is intense. But I can feel the unrest with the animals within myself." Ethan looked worried.

"I can feel all those things too." I said. "I could smell fear on Mom earlier." I chuckled.

"I know, me too. I smelled it on my dad after we came back from the clearing. It was like nothing I have ever smelled before. Like a new scent." Ethan was relieved it wasn't just him smelling fear.

"I know! I guess it makes sense." I shrugged.

"God, it's almost 5am. I better get home. If my dad sees I'm gone, especially after earlier, he's gonna flip out." Ethan looked so cozy in my bed. I knew he didn't want to go.

"I know. And if my mom finds you in my bed, that could be... awkward." I laughed.

"Hey we're only trying to save Emerald Lake. Totally innocent." Ethan smiled. "Anya. Why do you have a pine scented candle in here? Are you like, not getting enough real pine scent or something." Ethan started poking and tickling me.

I started laughing trying to avoid his tickles. "It was from Robin. I swear. A joke." I could barely speak; I was laughing but also trying not to make a sound, so it came out like I was snorting.

Ethan hugged me. His face pulled back and looked into my eyes closely. "I have to go." Just then he gently kissed me goodbye. My stomach jumped. "Try and get some sleep. I'll see you later." Ethan slid out of my bed, his face flushed. I wasn't sure I could form words yet, but somehow I squeaked out an "OK."

Ethan opened the door to the deck quietly. The storm had calmed some. "Lock the door behind me. You don't know what other animals might try and get into your bedroom," he joked.

I got out of bed and closed and locked the door behind him. I looked down at Fancy Beast poking her head out from under the bed. Out the window, I could see Ethan in his eagle form flying out over the lake. He looked so free and graceful. I watched him soar through the air and disappear over the trees heading home. I think I probably loved him.

10

STRESS PANCAKES

School was canceled until further notice, as the power was out in the surrounding areas. Luckily, we still had electricity. I slept in later than I had in a long time; Mom and Auntie Lily slept in too. Everyone was wiped out from the late night.

Still in my pajamas, I went downstairs to make coffee. No one was up yet. I built a fire in the kitchen fireplace and drank a cup of coffee as I stared out the window at the lake. The sky had cleared from the night before, showing a cold sun. Snow was piled up high in all directions.

There was an old, bulky TV in the kitchen that I had ignored since moving in. I turned it on, curious if it even worked. Success! I switched through the channels with an actual dial—all three of them!—and looked for any local news that had reported on the storm damage. The picture was bad, and I noticed a silver telescoping rod on top. Oh God, an antenna! I pulled it out, setting it this way and that until the picture improved.

I made myself some cereal, and sat at the table watching the news anchors talk about the weather forecast for the next week. They talked about the weird weather and went over the school closures and the power outages. One poor reporter was bundled up and red-faced, out in the field looking miserably cold, as he pointed to downed power lines and trees. A snowplow did a good job trying to drown out his voice in the background. As the reporter started screaming over the snowplow, the station cut to a commercial. Dan Gann the Souvenir Man! In addition to bad souvenirs he apparently offered van tours of Emerald Lake, ending at the local casino CalNeva.

I shut off the TV and rubbed my eyes, turning my head quickly as something caught my eye. A raccoon was standing on the deck railing, hopping from foot to foot, his little hands splayed out in a sort of jazz-hands greeting.

My God, it was Jimmy! I rushed to the back door to open it, but by the time I got there, human Jimmy entered, along with a considerable amount of snowdrift.

"Hey!" He beamed. He noticed the pile of snow on the floor. "Oops," he said, "I need coffee." He then marched over the pile and into the kitchen, jolly.

"Jimmy! Don't worry about it," I said, in spite of his lack of worry. "Come inside. I just made some." I smiled.

Jimmy brushed the snow off of his fluffy mullet and stood in front of the fireplace warming his hands. "This shapeshifting business is really underrated. It's so easy to get around."

"Underrated by whom?" I snorted, laughing, as I poured him a cup of coffee.

Jimmy considered this. "Good point." He took the coffee mug and immediately started downing the brew. "So that was completely and utterly insane last night."

"I don't even know how to process it." I replied, pouring myself cup number three.

"I was thinking, later we need to shift and meet at the fracking site. If we check it out as our theriotypes, we can spy on it without being detected." Jimmy was focused and serious.

"Good. Yes. Agree. If we're going to stop it, we need to get eyes on it. Do you feel different now?" I probed.

"Very. My senses are so sharp. I'm different. I can feel people in ways I never could before. I usually can't read anyone, now I can read them completely. It's refreshing." Jimmy sat down at the table with his coffee.

I heard a shuffling from the hallway and Auntie Lily came into the kitchen in one of mom's robes, her hair a little wild.

"We all had a late sleep." Auntie Lily smiled.

"Good morning, Auntie Lily," Jimmy said.

Auntie Lily sat at the table next to Jimmy. "Can someone make an old lady some tea?"

"Yes, I can make you tea, Auntie." I smiled.

The cabin began to shake, but this time violently. Jimmy grabbed onto Auntie Lily and I steadied myself in the door jamb, as everything in the cupboards rattled. A glass pitcher fell off the shelf and broke. Fancy Beast ran into the other room, her eyes like saucers.

"Whoa. That was a big one." I whispered, almost afraid to talk.

Just then, we heard dogs and coyotes all barking and howling. I ran to the backdoor and opened it to hear better. The noise was so loud from the animals barking and howling, as if every canine, wolf, and coyote was yelling at once, screaming in protest. I could feel their discomfort. It echoed across the lake and through the trees, over the homes and around all of Emerald.

Mom came running into the kitchen, looking half awake.

"What is going on!? What broke?" She looked crazed.

"Just a pitcher. The animals are disturbed." Auntie Lily looked out the window. "It's not good."

Far in the distance, the horizon of the lake seemed to lift and settle. I drew nearer to the window. After a moment, long, smooth waves began to ripple out from the center of the lake, as though someone had dropped a gigantic stone in it. "OK, that's weird," I said softly. Lily looked grave.

Mom pulled her hair back into a bun. "Who wants pancakes?!" she cried, completely ignoring the quake, the lake, and our grim expressions.

"Oh, I do!" Jimmy raised a hand like he was in class.

Auntie Lily and I exchanged a look.

"Oh, pancakes will fix everything!" I felt bad immediately after saying it, but I couldn't help myself.

"What do you want me to do? I can't control the frackers or stop the Earth from shaking. But I can make pancakes, OK?" She banged around in the cupboards, getting out a large mixing bowl. "Why don't you clean up the glass that broke," she ordered, annoyed.

As I threw away chunks of pitcher and swept up the glass dust, I could hear the animals' howls subside. I stared out the window at the lake, thinking about what was coming, and how we were not even close to being prepared. I looked up and saw an eagle flying circles around the cabin. It was Ethan. I could feel him. Jimmy could too.

"Jimmy, you wanna come hang out in my room, while Mom makes pancakes for us? I want to show you a cool painting of my grandma's." I lured Jimmy upstairs.

"Sure. I love Grandma Mae's paintings." Jimmy was up from the table in a flash, and followed me out of the kitchen.

"Don't be too long, breakfast will be ready in about fifteen minutes." Mom yelled to us as we left the room.

We climbed the stairs to my room. "Did you see Ethan?" I asked quietly.

"Yeah, let's get him inside," Jimmy urged as we went into my room.

"Can you open the door for him? I'm going to get dressed."

I grabbed some clothes from the dresser and went into the bathroom. Jimmy looked out the window and saw Ethan standing on the deck, pacing.

I came out of the bathroom and both Jimmy and Ethan were sitting on the bed, looking at the book. "This is incredible," Jimmy paged through the illustrations in awe.

"I flew over the lake, low. I went far out to the middle and there is definitely something going on. The water is choppy from the storm, but there's like a huge, circular ripple that is continuously pulsating out." Ethan said.

"We saw," I said. "It's the Watanuuk, isn't it?"

We sat in silence for a moment, knowing I was right but not having a clue what to do about it.

"I think there is some ritual the Tuhánee did, sealing the Watanuuk to the nest. I can feel it cracking open. I don't know how much time we have, but Jimmy suggested we shift and go check out the fracking site; see what is happening over there." I pulled my hair back into a tight ponytail.

"Yeah. Let's not get everyone out there. It might be too much. Let's have just the three of us go so we can be stealth. Then we can report back to the pack," Ethan suggested.

"That makes sense," Jimmy said, "Let's eat pancakes and go do this!"

"Pancakes!?" Ethan hopped up, delighted.

After breakfast we told Mom we were going to hike around exploring. Naturally, she urged us not to get lost in any storms and to be back before five o'clock. We all nodded vigorously.

Jimmy, Ethan and I walked from the cabin down our street and headed towards Ruby Trailhead. It was a pleasant, long walk. Once at the trails, we could easily shift without being detected. The fracking was set up someplace near Eagle Lake, I remembered, and once I was in cat form I was sure I could find it.

We entered the trail, and the walk was so peaceful and quiet. The storm did a lot of damage, with fallen trees everywhere and loads of snow piled high, but we were able to navigate everything and hike OK. A few people were out walking and backpacking, but it was fairly quiet. A couple came toward us down the trail with their black lab; he seemed extremely interested in smelling me. He sniffed me with great enthusiasm. I could sense his thoughts. *Cat. Person. Cat. Big cat? Person??* He looked at me, bewildered, and it was all I could do not to laugh.

"Wow, Hunter is fascinated by you," the man said. The dog kept gingerly poking his head at me for cautious sniffs.

"He's probably smelling my cat," I said. I heard Jimmy snort, almost spitting out his water.

The couple tugged the dog along the trail as the poor thing stared after us with the same confused expression. *It's OK*, I told him, in my new way. He started jumping up and barking, and continued until the couple had dragged him out of earshot.

We continued walking; Ethan was distracted. He was quiet, which was unusual for him.

"Are you OK?" I asked him, concerned.

"There's something going on at the fracking site. I'm getting some feelings from the other birds over there. I don't know how to describe it." Ethan said concerned.

"Oh you don't have to explain it, I know exactly what you mean. But what do you think is happening? I'm not really getting anything." I stopped to tie my shoe. Jimmy sat on a rock and drank some water. He passed the container to me and I took a swig.

"I'm not sure exactly but I think we should shift up here, back behind these boulders. If we get separated after we look at the fracking site, meet back here and we'll hike back in human form, OK?" Ethan instructed.

"Sounds good," Jimmy said.

"Copy that," I agreed.

We walked behind a huge set of boulders and joined hands. Each of us closed our eyes and envisioned our animals next to us. Within seconds I felt one with the mountain lions again, and no longer could feel Jimmy and Ethan's hands. My entire vision changed, and I was in lion form.

Jimmy was next to me in his raccoon body. He hopped on my back, knowing I could carry him farther and faster than if he were to run on his own.

I saw Ethan high above us, flying in circles, waiting for us to follow. The cold snow felt so good on my four feet. The thrill of having all this power and strength, to run and jump off of boulders and up mountains, was intoxicating. I showed off some, and darted really fast up and around the trees, keeping track of Ethan above. I could feel Jimmy's elation as I leaped off of rocks and over fallen trees. I was now up fairly high, and could see Eagle Lake in the distance.

Ethan was well ahead of us, and making his way towards the fracking setup. There were two large construction cranes, lots of trucks, and a number of structures, some of them looking like a tangle of pipes, whose purpose wasn't clear. I raced down the mountain towards the clearing, where Ethan was doing lazy circles in the sky, waiting for us to catch up.

In no time we were on the perimeter of the operation. There were tons of hoses everywhere, and these big upright tanks set up in groups of four. There was chain-link fencing around the area, but Jimmy was able to sneak underneath it easily. I snagged a link with one of my giant, fearsome claws and pulled, watching the links pop free one by one until I could walk right through.

I could see several workmen in the distance, busily tending to the mass of machinery. I hung back in the trees. Ethan was perched really close to the action. I saw a few workers stop and look at him, then go back to their tasks. Jimmy was slowly making his way closer to the trucks to get a better look. I knew if anyone saw me, there would be a freakout, so I definitely wanted to stay undetected.

Well, Well, Well LLC was printed on a banner that was displayed on some of the fencing, with the warning KEEP OUT. PRIVATE PROP-ERTY. I climbed one of the tall pine trees and was able to steady myself on a large branch to get a better look. Camouflaged in the branches, no one noticed me.

I saw the entrance gate open and a van, decked out with a colorful promotional wrap, drove in. I could make out the cartoon Dan Gann and his plaid sport coat on the side, and then the real Dan Gann behind the wheel, in a different plaid sport coat. What the heck was he doing here?

The van parked and Dan trundled out, clapping a hard hat onto his head. Several men walked out of an office trailer, and they all stopped to talk. Dan was animated in a goofy and excitable way. The young guys he was talking to I assumed were managers, except they were dressed in track suits, and looked more like gangsters than business-men. The ground shook slightly; one of the trucks was pumping something into the ground.

I looked up at Ethan in the tree. He was watching Dan carefully. One of the tracksuit guys gave him a briefcase, they shook hands, and Dan did a ridiculous bow and got back into his van.

As the van drove out through the gate, I could sense Ethan was ready to leave. We'd seen enough. Ethan flew off over the trees and towards the trails.

Jimmy and I connected and he hopped back on me as we made our way back to the boulders at the trails. The transition from animal to human always surprises me—it's so smooth and easy. Jimmy and I sat on a rock drinking water and waiting on Ethan.

"So what's the deal with you and Ethan?" Jimmy probed.

"What do you mean, deal?" I asked, flustered.

"You know what I mean. He likes you." Jimmy smiled mischievously.

I am fairly sure I turned multiple shades of red and before I could answer, Ethan was walking towards us. Jimmy pointed two fingers at his eyes and then at mine, indicating he was keeping his eyes on me.

"OK, so that was interesting." Ethan was a little out of breath and sat down on the rock next to me. He took the water bottle from my hand and guzzled.

"Yeah, what the heck was Dan Gann doing there?" I asked accusatorially.

"That guy is nothing but shady. He's got crook energy," Jimmy stated.

"He's ridiculous." I laughed.

"My grandmother had words with him at his pathetic shack years ago. Get this, she and Auntie Lily were going to sell him some Tuhánee art—baskets and some belts for his business. He asked for one example to look at, kept 'em, then had them knocked off at some Chinese factory." Jimmy was fired up. "Now he sells knockoff Tuhánee art, as well as stupid t-shirts and knick-knacks."

"Yeah he sucks overall, but there's more going on with him. I just don't know what yet." Ethan was pensive.

"We better get back." I noticed the sun was rapidly setting, and I didn't want to worry Mom again. The hike took a while in human form and we had a ways to go.

We all started walking back the way we came, around Ruby Trailhead and heading towards Pine Needle Way. The sun reflecting off the lake. Ethan stopped us.

He pointed far out to the middle of the lake. "Look, it's happening again." We saw the same weird rise and fall, as though the water were a blanket being lifted from underneath, and the same huge ripples, emanating from the center.

"Do you guys feel the same strange new feeling when you see it? Like a glitchy feeling?" I said, unnerved. They both nodded, not taking their eyes off the lake.

"The Watanuuk's coming soon, isn't it?" I almost whispered.

Our silence said it all.

"I'm going to get the others over tomorrow and we can fill them in. School, I guess, is still canceled until they fix the power lines. Anya, can you bring your book to show everyone?" Ethan asked.

"Of course." As we approached my house, I kneeled down and picked up a fat pinecone. I felt a need to try something. I chucked the pinecone as far as I could, which apparently was exceptionally far!

"Wow great arm, Girl!" Ethan was impressed. The pinecone exploded off a tree, the very one I'd been aiming at.

"Ha! More new abilities unlocked," I laughed, looking up at the pink skies. "Guys, so do you think time speeds up when we are shifted, or are we just having so much fun we lose track of time?"

"I think we lose track of time. I mean, none of us are that great with time management anyways, right?" Jimmy was jogging backwards towards the cabin, his raccoon makeup glistening in the sunset sky.

"That's the truth." Ethan rubbed his hands together, chilly.

"Mom should have the fireplace lit, if you want to warm up inside." I was hopping up each step of the cabin to shake the snow off my boots.

I opened the door, and standing in front of the fireplace warming herself, was Robin.

11

ROBIN

I stood in the doorway in total shock.

"AAAHHHHHHHHHHH!!!" Robin's booming voice screamed and echoed through the cabin as she ran over to me and hugged me tightly, spinning me around in circles. The boys took a step back, startled.

"Whoa, this must be Robin!" Ethan laughed. "Geez, kid, you *are* loud."

"Hey, you better believe I'm loud!" Robin stopped hugging me and walked right up to Ethan. "Are you Ethan?"

"This is Ethan and Jimmy." I introduced Robin to them as they came into the living room, shutting the door, keeping the cold air out.

"How?! How are you here!?" I kept hugging Robin.

"I'm only here until tomorrow night. My dad has a conference in Silver Run, and I told him if he didn't bring me to see you I'd make his life a living nightmare. So I called your mom yesterday to ask if I could surprise you." Robin was looking around the cabin at all the art. "This place is incredible."

Mom walked into the living room smiling from ear to ear, carrying a tray with cupcakes and coffee.

"Can you believe it! Our Robin is HERE! And it's so lucky you missed the freak storm." Mom placed the tray on the coffee table as everyone descended on the cupcakes like wild animals.

"Ohh, these are so good." Ethan jammed the whole cupcake in his mouth. Jimmy was pouring the coffee for everyone.

"Was there a play?" Robin was looking at Jimmy's face.

"No, no, he's just part raccoon." I said matter-of-factly.

"Of course he is." Robin took the coffee from Jimmy. "Are you *all* raccoons, or?" Robin lifted an eyebrow.

"No, just Jimmy." Ethan smirked.

"So what do you want to do while you're here, Robin?" Mom asked, hoping to help plan things.

"I want to see everything!" Robin beamed. "Starting with your room and the lake."

"Hey, we're gonna take off. You two catch up. I gotta call the pack and..." Ethan trailed off from his thought.

"Pack?" Nothing got by Robin.

"Pack of pals." Jimmy interjected. "Yeah, we better get going. Robin, I hope we see you later—maybe we can go snowboarding while you're here!" Jimmy hugged Robin.

"Oh, I love snowboarding. I may wanna come back sooner than later and actually spend some time here. So yes, next time for sure." Robin was so happy.

Ethan smiled wide as he walked backwards out the door, waving cutely. "See ya later."

I waved back as the boys left. "Come on, let me show you my room. You're gonna love it." I grabbed Robin's duffle bag and started up the stairs. Mom was so elated seeing us together. She gathered the empty tray and headed back to the kitchen. Fancy Beast was at the top of the stairs, glaring at Robin. She let out a small hiss.

"Glad to see you too, Fancy Creep." Robin hissed.

"Be nice, you two." I laughed.

I flung open the door to my room and proudly presented all that was mine. "Behold! My vintage room."

Robin looked at everything like she was an inspector. She ran into the bathroom, looked under the bed, opened the closet and messed with the typewriter. She jumped on the chair and sat in it on her knees, looking out at the lake. The wind was howling and the snow was still piled high from the storm.

"This is an upgrade for sure. And look at all these books!" Robin smiled, pulling random books off the shelf. "And Ethan?" Robin fanned herself with a book, like she was passing out.

"You think he's cute?" I was eager for her approval.

"Are you kidding me? He's gorgeous. And he clearly likes you. I need to move here. Does he have a brother?" Robin was playfully envious. Her bag was on my bed. She unzipped it, pulled out a brochure, and handed it to me. "Dude, we have to do this. It looks so incredibly bad it might be good. Plus, I want to see as much as I can while I'm here for ONE whole day." I took the brochure from Robin. It was a discount flyer for a van tour of Emerald Lake from Dan Gann the Souvenir Man. The Universe was at work here, and I couldn't ignore it.

"Where did you get this?" I asked curiously.

"Oh, the Uber driver had it in the backseat of his car." Robin shrugged.

"That's clever. OK then, I'll sign us up." I snapped the QR code on the flyer and made reservations for the next morning.

Just then my phone dinged with that odd school alert, stating school would be back in session, starting Monday.

"What was that?" Robin was looking at my phone.

"Oh, the school district sends out these text alerts when the school is closed. We get snow days and stuff here. After the freaky storm the power lines were damaged at school, so we didn't have to go. But it's been fixed so back at it Monday." I grimaced.

Robin opened my door to the deck and went outside, taking in the incredible views. The sun had just set and the stars were coming out. The night was clear and cold. "It smells like fireplaces. Hey, I'm gonna go check out the lake. I'll be right back." Robin yelled as she started down the stairs.

"Wait, not alone!" I was thinking about the Watanuuk and the legend.

"What? Why? Serial killer loose?" Robin asked, alarmed.

"No. Just... I wanna come too. Let me grab my sweater. Wait for me. Don't go without me." Robin stopped in her tracks and waited on me to join her.

We walked down by the lake, crunching through the fresh snow. Just then, the earth shook.

"Whoa, earthquake!" Robin exclaimed.

"Yeah, we have been getting a lot of those lately. It's from the fracking." I informed her.

"Who would frack here? That seems illegal and stupid." Robin looked sickened by the thought.

"Yeah, it's messy." I shook my head. We walked back towards the cabin and Robin ventured out onto the pier. There were a few dead frozen fish on it from the other day. Robin curiously kicked one of the fish, sending it spinning like a top.

"Weird! What happened to these poor guys?"

I paused for a moment. How to get into it? "The fish were acting really strange right before the storm. They must have known things were about to get weird?"

I was relieved when Robin suddenly noticed the boathouse.

"Ohhh a boat! Can we use it this summer?" Robin was excited. "Because I have already decided to live here all summer with you," Robin schemed.

"Yes, we can use it! Party on the lake." I was starting to feel so much calmer having Robin here. As I looked around in the dark, I could see everything. My night vision was superb. I watched Robin jumping around and dancing on the shoreline, crunching ice with her snow boots. I wasn't sure how to tell her about all that had happened. She was my best friend, but everything that had gone down was so crazy, and she was only here for a day. Maybe I would wait until she came back for longer. It seemed like a conversation that needed to be handled with finesse.

"I am so hungry and I miss your mom's cooking. Can we go in and force her to cook us that chicken thing she does?" Robin was skipping back towards the house.

"Oh my God, the chicken and cheese enchilada casserole?" I was hungry too.

"That's the one." Robin was climbing the stairs to my deck when an eagle swooped down and landed on the railing. "GAHHHHH!" Robin startled, and almost fell backwards. It was Ethan. I looked at Ethan and shook my head no, doing the cut gesture across my neck. Ethan launched off the railing and flew right over me soaring over the lake. As all this happened in a split second, I had somehow gotten from the end of the pier to right behind Robin to catch her so she didn't get hurt. She landed in my arms. I had the quickness and dexterity of my mountain lion form, in human Anya form.

"How did you do that?!" Robin was delighted, yet baffled. I was delighted Ethan didn't shift right in front of us.

"I'm fast." I joked. I noticed a strange odor coming off of Robin. It wasn't the fear I had smelled on Mom, but a new scent that I had never experienced before. I was trying to identify it, but I had no reference. It wasn't sweet or sour. It was almost a new category. If I had to guess, it was probably the smell of her adrenaline.

After Mom's chicken dinner and dessert, I set Robin up in the room next to mine. It was smaller than my room, with no deck, but it had huge windows with beautiful views. There were two twin beds and several lake paintings on the wall. I had barely explored this room, but noticed an old framed photograph on the wall of my Grandmother Mae, Auntie Lily, and Frederick with his wife Sue, my great, great grandmother. They were well dressed in traditional clothing, and were standing in front of the lake in a typical vintage family-photo stance. They stood, unsmiling, down by where the pier would have been, but it clearly wasn't built yet. Grandma Mae must have been 13 or 14 years old, Auntie Lily still a toddler. The lake looked similar in the photo but the trees were smaller. I strained and looked closer, noticing the mountain-lion ring on Frederick's finger.

"This is a great room. This whole place is just so..... cozy." Robin beamed.

"Yeah, and if you get lonely, the closets connect us." I explained.

"What? How cool." Robin immediately opened the closet door, noticing the small door at the back of her closet. "The door is so small." She was crawling to the back to investigate.

Not much was in the closet, just two old boxes and nothing hanging up but a black puffer jacket. Robin opened the door and the weird smell came lofting into the bedroom.

"Oh God, it smells like a museum." Robin was holding her hand over her mouth.

"Yeah, I don't think much airflow has been in there for some time."

"Whoa, it's filled with paintings." Robin was picking through the canvases stacked along the walls. "Who painted all of these? They're all over the cabin."

"My Grandma Mae was an artist. She painted all the time and did all these paintings of the lake. My Auntie Lily, her younger sister, does a lot of basket art. My mom is re-learning the old Tuhánee basket weaving." I said, crouched in the closet, starting to open some of the boxes.

"That's good for your mom. She needs a hobby now that she is single." Robin had crawled back out of the inner closet and was watching me poke around the boxes.

"What's in there?"

"Let's see." I shrugged with lifted eyebrows excitedly.

On the side of one of the boxes was scribbled *Mary* in light pencil. I tore off the discolored tape and flipped open the dusty lid. Inside I found handmade masks, much like the masks I found in the closet in my room. They reminded me of the therian masks the pack were making at Ethan's. In the box was mask after mask of deer, all different and beautifully made. I pulled one out and put it to my face. Robin did the same. We got up and danced around the room in our deer masks. "Oh deer, my face." Robin laughed. "Deer me. I need to put on my make up." I laughed. "Be a deer and get me a soda?" Robin was laughing so hard she could barely talk.

"My God, we're stupid. Did your mom make these?" Robin asked, out of breath from just the few minutes of dancing.

"I think so." I pushed the mask up over my head. I sat on the end of the bed, thinking about the deer we saw the day we drove into town. How it jumped in front of our car. It must be Mom's theriotype!

"I am so out of breath and tired." Robin fell back on the end of the bed exhausted, mask still on her face.

"It's the altitude. You won't be here long enough to acclimate." I told her, lost in thought.

"Can I take a bath in your amazing tub? I think I wanna hit the sack early so we can explore tomorrow." Robin was up and mask off.

"Only if you use the secret passageway to get to my room." I laughed.

"Done." Robin scurried through the open closet doors to my room.

I checked my phone and saw a missed text from Ethan.

Sorry about that. I wasn't sure if you told her.
I wanted to dazzle her with my Eagle
greatness.

It's OK. I will tell her, but I think I will wait until we have more time together. Kinda a lot to throw on her for like a 24 hour visit. I might wait til she comes during the summer. She wants to go on the Dan Gann Van tour tomorrow.

Really? That should be interesting.

She loves dumb stuff. 

I waited, nervous about the heart emoji part.

Ethan sent a heart back.

. . .

I was complete.

I put the masks back into the box and pushed it back against the wall of the closet. There was another, older box in there that said *Sue* on it. It was smaller than the mask box. I pulled it close to me. I could hear the pipes squeaking as Robin filled the tub. I blew dust off the top as I unfolded the four flaps. Inside, I found a small cloth folded up, and inside of that silver cuff bracelets with colorful stones set into them. There were two of them. I turned them around in my hand admiring them and tried one on. Then I folded them back up in the cloth and placed them aside. Next, I picked up a small Tuhánee- style basket with a lid. I took off the lid and inside a beaded belt was neatly rolled up. I uncoiled it, and it had a pattern of arrows in blue and yellow and white, and in the center a large bird with wings outstretched. I kept digging around in the box, and pulled out a small leather vest with some fringe and an eagle feather. At the very bottom of the box was a really old envelope, and inside, a drawing showing the necklace with the eagle stone. The same necklace that is in the book with all the illustrations! I looked at the back of the drawing and written in what I assumed was Tuhánee were a bunch of words I didn't know. It looked like a list. I needed to show this to Jimmy and Auntie Lily later. I stuffed the envelope in my pocket.

Robin popped back into the closet. "Hey, what are you doing?" She had a towel wrapped up around her head, turban style. She had found my robe.

"Ah, just looking at old stuff." I carefully put the rest of the items back into the box and shoved them against the wall. I crawled back through the closet passageway and into my room.

"I want to stay up and talk to you all night but I am so tired. I'm not gonna make it, Anya. I got out of the tub so fast cause I was falling asleep." Robin was unraveling the turban and shaking her hair all over the place to dry it out.

"We have *all* day tomorrow. Get some sleep and we'll see everything you want. I'm so glad you're here." I hugged Robin tight and pushed her at the closet. "Go. Bed. Sleep."

Robin laughed and disappeared into the mysteriously cool closet passageway. "Good night!" She was louder than necessary- as always.

I decided I didn't feel like a bath, so I just put on my pajamas and got under the covers. Fancy Beast came out from under my bed to cuddle with me, thankful Robin was in the other room. The clock read 11:47PM. I wasn't tired. I found myself having trouble sleeping at night, but feeling like naps during the day time. I think my human and feline dualities were battling it out, with the catnaps winning.

I could hear Mom downstairs running the dishwasher and tidying up. She was still awake, always puttering. I put on my headphones, listening to music as I tried to summon sleep. As I was drifting off, my phone vibrated. The Discord thread with the pack was firing off messages furiously. I flung the headphones off my head and read the feed. It was filled with photos.

Guys look at what's outside my house! Terra had added a video to the chat. It was their front yard, but I couldn't understand what I was seeing. It slowly dawned on me: it was filled with wolves. All standing quietly and looking directly at Terra's window. The video went on for some time, panning back and forth, but the wolves just stood there.

Faye's message was next.

Something is happening. Look!! Faye's video showed a dozen bears, standing on their hind legs, staring.

Ethan's photo showed a bunch of eagles—maybe fifty?—all lined up in the backyard and across the deck.

Lucy had hundreds of squirrels on her roof.

Felix and Jimmy were at Felix's house, where his yard was full of deer and raccoons. All quietly standing together, looking into the window of Felix's room.

Iris's text was last: *What is going on?* A photo of her yard included tons of foxes, all laying down and looking at her through the sliding door.

I jumped out of bed and looked out the window. I couldn't see much with the reflection of the interior lights, so I opened the door and went out on the deck. Along the shoreline, lined up on the pier, were mountain lions. Easily twenty-five mountain lions, all sitting upright and looking up at my window, silent and still. I took a photo and added it to the Discord. I immediately knew why they were there. It was a warning.

12

BURIED

Morning hit me hard. I didn't sleep well with the whole late-night lion-visit situation, but needless to say, I was ready for a fun day with my best pal. I was still in bed, but it was fairly early so I figured I'd try and sleep another half an hour. I had just closed my eyes when the closet door flew open. Robin burst into song:

"Wakey Wakey eggs n' bakey

No mistakey, here's the dawn

Eyes are open, full of hopin', no more mopin'

Stretch and yawn!

She had her deer mask on, dancing wildly in her pajamas, her blonde hair sticking out of the sides of the mask.

All I could do was laugh. Robin could make me laugh in my worst mood. I jumped out of bed, joining her in the ridiculous dance.

"So we have to be at the souvenir shop in two hours. That gives us just enough time to eat breakfast and get ready." Robin pushed her mask on top of her head and looked outside at the lake. "Dude, what are all those footprints?" She pointed; the entire lakefront around the pier was covered in mountain lion tracks, the fresh snow pushed down and melted right to the ground.

"Oh wow, looks like an animal visited last night." I played it off like it was no big deal.

"It looks like an entire busload of animals visited. Is that normal?" Robin looked concerned.

"I mean, not really. I didn't hear anything, did you?" I wasn't lying.

"No, I slept like the dead. Weird." Robin pushed her mask back down and went through the closet. "Get ready, Mountain Girl."

After breakfast, Mom was surprisingly chipper to drive us to Dan Gann's. She actually got the irony of our desire to take the tour.

"Call me when you need to be picked up. Robin, your dad texted me; he's sending the Uber to our house at seven, then he's going to meet you at the airport for your late flight."

"Sounds good. That means we have exactly ten hours together. Let's cram as much fun as we can into the day." Robin jumped out of the car, full of energy.

I hopped out, excited to see Emerald too. Even though Dan Gann was obviously a cheese log, there was a lot I still hadn't seen of my new home town.

Mom drove off and we walked over to the souvenir shack. The wrapped van I had seen at the fracking site was parked out front. We were instructed to be there by 9AM sharp. We walked inside, right on time. The bells on the door clanged horribly. I was surprised no one else was there yet, but behind the counter was Dan Gann. I wondered where Russell might be. Dan was on the phone texting. He didn't even look up to greet us.

Robin walked around the little shop, pointing out stupid Emerald touristy keychains and shirts with trite slogans like My Mom Went to Emerald Lake and All I Got Was This Dumb T- Shirt.

The "Tuhánee" baskets were in. I picked one up and turned it over. MADE IN CHINA was on a little sticker at the bottom. I felt slimy even touching it. Robin walked up to Dan.

"Excuse me, are you who we check in with? We're taking the tour." Dan, noticeably startled by Robin's loud voice, dropped his phone.

"Well good morning to you. Yes, I am the person to check in with, thank you. I'm Dan Gann. Unfortunately, the guy that gives the tours, Andy, decided to quit with no notice. How thoughtful huh? I guess no one wants to work anymore. So I'll be driving that fancy van today." Dan picked his phone up and extended a cornball hand to instigate a shake. Robin obliged.

"I'm Robin and this is Anya. Where are the others?" Robin asked, looking around the shack, noticing no one else.

"Today it's just us. A quiet tour, so you lucky ladies get me all to your-selves!" Dan flashed a yellow-toothed grin; he had a big gap between his front two teeth. "Ladies, I will heat up the van. Stay in here a few minutes, and once the van is sufficiently warmed up we will head out on our adventure, posthaste!" Robin shot me a glance; the cheese factor was already promisingly high.

I walked back towards the far end of the shop, near the discounted items. There was a door that said EMPLOYEES ONLY. Dan was out front getting the van situated, so I did what any natural snoop would do: I opened the door and walked inside.

"What are you doing?" Robin whispered, completely surprised at my rebellion.

"Shhhh.. I'll be right back." I said, as I poked my head out the door. Inside the small back room there were shelves with knockoff merchandise, boxes of t-shirts, and several large, dusty carved wooden bears piled in the corner. A cold wind was blowing in through a small window where one of the panes was broken. It had been sealed with clear packing tape, but the tape had come loose from the dusty sill and it flapped in the wind. The room was fairly packed, and there was another door next to a messy desk, piled high with receipts and file folders. The door had one of those keypad entry locks, but it had been left slightly opened. I pushed the door slowly open to see what was inside. I got a glimpse of glass display cabinets, and what looked like expensive jewelry and antiques.

Just as I was about to venture in, the door from the shop opened up and Dan was standing there.

"Can I help you?!" His annoyance strained against his politeness.

"Oh, I was looking for the restroom. I needed to go before our adventure." I laughed nervously.

"Well it's not back here. I have a key at the front desk I'll give you. The bathroom is outside around the back." Dan was gesturing in a hurried manner for me to leave the Employees Only area. He was obviously very uncomfortable with me poking around.

"Oh great, thanks so much. Sorry about that, I thought the bathroom might be back here." I played it off as embarrassment.

"Nope." Dan gave a terse grimace which I assumed was meant to be a grin.

Robin looked at me with wide eyes and gestured a confused *sorry* for somehow not warning me Dan was on his way to bust me. I waved it off; no biggie.

"I need to use the restroom. Do you need to go too?" I asked Robin, as I took the key from Dan. The key was attached to a giant soup ladle, apparently to keep the unwashed masses from stealing this incredibly valuable junk-shop bathroom access.

"Yes, yes I do." Robin and I scooted out of the shop and around the back of the shack.

"What were you doing back there?" Robin whispered, genuinely concerned.

"I was just curious. And I do have to go to the bathroom." I opened the bathroom door; the ladle slammed against the doorjamb. It was about what I expected. Gas-station toilet elegant.

After returning the key to Dan, we were ready for the tour. The van was actually pretty decent, and we buckled up looking forward to seeing more of the Emerald area.

The tour began in Pine Crest, and our first stop was to see the Penny Bear. It's a Burning Man art sculpture of a bear and her cubs, all made of pennies. They call her Ursa Mater. I couldn't help but wonder how many photos Faye had of this bear, and snapped a selfie in front of Penny to send her.

We got back into the van and slowly went along the highway. Notable points of interest were shared, and Dan Gann elaborated with painful puns and terrible jokes. He told us about a show called Bonanza that was filmed in Emerald. I had never heard of it, but apparently it was important? He talked about Bonanza a lot, and I prayed to any God listening for him to stop talking about Bonanza. He even recited his favorite episode in great detail where some character named Hoss was wrongfully accused of robbing a bank and was almost hung. My God. Please stop.

But wait, not before more fun facts about the lake—"It's 10,000 years old, only slightly older than me, hahahhaha. It's the second deepest lake in the world and it's the largest alpine lake in North America," Dan prattled on. I could see why we were the only two people on this stupid van. I could tell Robin was now wishing we were snowboarding, but we kept exchanging humorous glances whenever Dan said anything dumb, which was pretty much constantly.

Once we passed Prince Beach we were almost at the Nevada border. Snow was falling at a faster rate. As soon as we passed the border Dan screamed "Welcome to NEVADA," but he used kind of a cowboy accent so it came out like *Nevady*. It startled the hell out of me. This set Robin off. She could not stop laughing. She was howling and holding her sides as tears streamed down her face. I caught the laughs, and was in agony with side pain from cracking up. Dan thought we just were amused by him, so he joined in the laughter, which made it all the more impossible to stop.

Finally, I composed myself.

"Dan Gann, are we going by Cave Rock?" I asked, still panting a little.

"We sure are... we're gonna cross over from Highway 18 over to 70 and we'll head through Cave Rock. We used to be able to climb it, but some locals pitched a fit. I guess they didn't want anyone having fun, so we can't do that no more." I swallowed my annoyance.

"Can we stop for a break there? I'd love to see it," I asked.

"We're gonna drive right through it, but we can stop and look around, no problem. They call it The Lady of the Lake. We're going all around the whole lake actually, ending with a stop at Jadeite Bay. I usually end at the casino, but you two can't gamble." Dan said, laughing.

"What's Cave Rock?" Robin asked me.

"I've heard a lot about it from Ethan and Jimmy. I just wanted to see it."

As we drove, I noticed the sky darkening with more clouds. In addition to the snow falling, the wind was really picking up. I could feel an animal uneasiness within myself. I tried to ignore it, but it was getting louder in my body.

"Are you OK?" Robin looked concerned as she handed me a water bottle. "Drink some water, you look pale."

"I think I'm just getting a little carsick with the winding roads." I took the water, sipping it gently. I wanted to tell Robin everything, but how do you do that on a van tour?

Oh hey, by the way Robin, since moving to Emerald Lake, all my friends and I turn into animals at will and can talk to other animals in our heads. We also might have to battle some legendary monster that lives in a nest at the bottom of the lake.

Yeah, this was gonna take a minute to explain.

Robin squeezed my hand. She looked at my ring.

"This is new?" She asked me.

"It's actually old. My great grandfather's ring." I smiled.

"It's super cool." Robin admired it, the blue sapphire glowing slightly. "Your mom never talked about her family." Robin pointed out.

"Yeah, I know. I just know about my dad's side and they were never all that friendly." I felt sad mentioning my dad.

"Screw him. Someday he'll be sorry. You'll see." Robin said confidently.

The van was swerving a little on the road, as the wind had really increased. I felt a lot colder. I looked at my phone, checking the weather app. The phone hadn't caught up with the real time weather yet, as it didn't even mention the wind.

I texted the Penny Bear photo to the Discord chat.

For you Faye—from my fantastic Dan Gann tour (insert sarcastic emoji here)

I caught up on the Discord conversations from the morning, mostly everyone complaining about feeling off. That was strange. I wasn't sure what was going on, but I knew it wasn't good.

"It's getting really stormy. Look at the snowfall." Robin was peering out the window at the darkening sky. "Should we maybe stop someplace?"

I looked out the window, and the storm was becoming a blizzard. It was like the freak storm from the other night. I started to feel strange. I could smell fear on Dan and it stunk, sour and oily.

"Dan..." I started.

"I can't..." He trailed off. The van wobbled in the wind. He was straining to look out the windshield; he brought his head down and to the center, to the point his chin almost touched the dash, straining to look up through the windshield at the mountainside to the right.

Suddenly, the van jerked to a stop! Robin and I lurched forward against our seatbelts, while Dan whipped his off. Almost before we could register what was happening, he opened the door and jumped out, the seatbelt warning going *Bong. Bong. Bong.* Robin and I watched in horror, craning our heads around as he ran off at top speed in the opposite direction. The van crept forward terrifyingly; it was still in gear, and the open driver door flapped in the wind. I spun around to see what had scared him. Just in time to see the wall of white.

With a sickening *WHUMP* the van was knocked sideways, instantly plunging us into a deep gray darkness. I felt the van slide all the way across the road and tip over the edge, throwing us crazily as the van fell hard on its side. It went even darker, and everything was silent except the *Bong. Bong. Bong. Bong* of the seatbelt alert.

I looked around. Was I dead? My ears were ringing. The front driver door was ripped off the van entirely, and snow was packed into the front-seat area. Robin and I were behind, in the front row of passenger seats. We were encased in almost complete darkness, but between the still-functioning dash lights and my new vision, I could see well.

I looked over at Robin, frantic; she was passed out and leaning against the far door, her seatbelt holding her in place. I could smell blood on her. I pulled her over towards me, but with the van on its side it was hard to maneuver. She had a cut on her forehead, and I dabbed it with my jacket sleeve. The van was completely buried in snow. How much, I had no idea. Luckily, I could tell I wasn't badly hurt. I checked my pocket for my phone and pulled it out. No bars. The alarm droned on idiotically: *Bong. Bong. Bong.*

"Robin! Robin, can you hear me!" I shook her. Nothing.

She was breathing, just out cold. I looked around, trying to figure a way out. I tried to open my door, but the snow was too heavy and it wouldn't budge. I thought I could try to get out through the front seat and out the driver's side, where the door had been. I unbuckled myself, crawling over to the front seat, and tried to dig. The snow was jammed around the steering wheel. My hands were so cold, and it was hard to steady myself with the van on its side. This would take forever and I wasn't strong enough.

Robin was starting to stir, moaning slightly. It was difficult to breathe and it occurred to me we had limited oxygen, but more importantly, Robin might be bleeding internally, and we were miles from help. I knew what I needed to do. I unbuckled Robin, then steadied myself in the front-seat area and focused my breathing. I called to my mountain lions, and saw us become one. Within seconds I had shifted. It was the first time I had done it alone.

The size of my cat form surprised me—I was suddenly filling almost the whole front-seat area. I maneuvered my hindquarters between the front seats, and leveraged my back paws against the rear seats so I was facing the windshield. I looked at the windshield, the faint glow of the headlights just barely visible through the packed snow. *How strong is a lion head?* I figured I was about to find out. Summoning all my quickness and strength, I pushed off of the rear seat and bashed my head full force into the windshield.

A mountain lion head, I discovered, was stronger than I'd feared, and I cracked through the safety glass like it was peanut brittle. Some snow poured in the hole, but to my relief, it stopped before filling much of the cab. With my great paws I started digging and pushing the snow straight out, the pebbly, jagged safety glass scratching me but not causing any real injury. It was hard, but I was able to make quick work of it. I was trying to dig a tunnel upwards, but I had no idea how much snow was on top of us or how deep we were buried. The freshness of the snow was causing it to fall back on me. I was digging feverishly, faster and faster; I knew time was not on our side.

As I continued to dig, I could hear the *Bong Bong Bong* becoming more and more muffled. I could hear digging above me! Someone had found us! Maybe it was the pack. I tried to connect to them, telling them where we were, asking for help. I could, faintly, hear Robin moaning and stirring. Above I saw frantic clawing at the snow, and a blinding circle of daylight appeared! The clawing stopped, and *WHOOSH!* a lion poked its face into the hole, steam pouring from its mouth and nostrils.

We locked eyes, and in an instant, we understood each other.

I wriggled up out of the hole; there was another lion there, panting out huge clouds of steam. They'd done a lot of digging already, but I'd kicked almost as much snow down in the hole as had been there to start, and we needed to widen it if I was going to drag Robin out backwards.

The three of us attacked the hole, a spray of snow flying up all around us. After a minute or so, it wasn't as wide as I would have liked, but I couldn't wait any longer.

I plunged in, digging downward, and made my way into the van. *Bong. Bong. Bong.* Robin moaned again; she was coming to. I bit into her coat, grabbing her tightly as I pulled her through to the front seat, and dragging her up through the snow. Her eyes opened and went very wide.

"aaaaAAAAAAAHHHHH!!!!" She screamed as she saw what was happening. She started to panic. I continued to pull her up through the snow, roughly—we didn't have time to be dainty about it. Robin's face was a mask of pure terror as she looked at me. All she saw was a mountain lion with a mouth full of her jacket, dragging her somewhere. She started to fight me, but I knew I had to get her further up so she could breathe. She was trying to scream and kick, which made pulling her out that much harder. But I did it. I was stronger, and I had her almost out of the snow, her face in daylight.

Just then, the snow from the pit we'd dug fell back in, burying her again. The two lions came to help; we madly dug after her and no sooner had we found her than Robin said, "nope nope nope nope nope," and started trying to clamber back down the hole into the van! I let out a big steamy lion sigh, and all three of us started digging, chasing her down the hole.

Finally, almost back in the van, I saw a hand. It looked as though the tunnel had collapsed and Robin was stuck. I gently but firmly took her hand in my mouth and pulled, while the other two lions dug.

As I pulled, it seemed like all the fight had gone out of poor Robin. She saw the other two lions, and her eyes went dead. I dragged her onto the top of the giant snowdrift, let her go, and looked in her eyes. She sat up. Then she looked straight at me and fainted. I felt awful, but I didn't have time to think about it.

The storm was raging. The lions stayed, watchful and eager to help. I settled myself and closed my eyes, asking to shift back, and asking for the pack to help. Instantly I was in my Anya body.

"Robin!!" I screamed.

I heard nothing. "Robin!!" I screamed again. "Wake up!!!"

Robin was coming to. "Anya." The smell of her fear was overpowering.

"Get up, help me." I yelled.

"A mountain lion tried to kill me!" She screamed.

"Use your feet. I'm getting you out of here."

I grabbed her by the back of her jacket and lifted her to her feet. The snow was falling fast. I looked around, my eyes sharp even in the blizzard. Then, of course, Robin noticed the lions.

"AAAAAHHHHH!!! They're HERE!!" The lions just sat there with worried looks on their faces.

"They're fine. It's no big deal. Come on. We need to go this way." I picked Robin up and steadied her. She was limping a little and just overall wobbly. I guided her towards a bus stop next to the road. Robin kept looking back at the lions in disbelief.

"Where are we going?" Robin was breathless, holding her side.

"Over here to get some shelter." I kept her upright.

"How can you see anything? Can't we just sit down for a minute?" Robin was woozy.

"No, we have to get under something, the storm is dangerous! Come on!" I draped her arm around my shoulder and carried her as best I could.

We got to the bus shelter and I took out my cell phone. One bar. I tried calling 911, but no luck. I tried Discord, but nothing was going through.

Then I focused and tried to connect to the pack. I could do it in mountain lion form; maybe I could as Anya. Did they hear me before? I sat still on the bus bench, freezing. Robin was in and out of consciousness, with her head propped against my shoulder. Another small avalanche had piled down the mountain about a hundred feet away. The road looked completely blocked. I scanned all around, unable to stop myself wondering where the heck Dan Gann had run off to. I could see emergency vehicle lights flashing in the distance. Maybe a plow?

"Hold on Robin... I think help is coming." I held her in my arms to generate heat, the wind blowing so fiercely it stung my face. I saw a shadow approaching in the thick snow. I couldn't quite make it out. As I squinted to get clarity I realized it was a bear. It was running towards us at top speed. It was Faye!

Faye came right up to us and squatted down at the bus bench. I knew she wanted me to get Robin on her back.

I shook Robin, waking her. She saw the bear and started to scream again. "aaaaaaAAAAAAAGHHHH!! Oh my God!!"

I held her face in my hands and looked directly into her eyes.

"You want to live, right?" I yelled.

"YES!" She cried.

"Don't ask me any questions now, but trust me. GET ON THE BACK OF THIS BEAR!!"

"WHATTTTTT!?" She was falling apart.

"Get on the bear and hold on! She won't hurt you." I had never looked more serious in my life. I stuck my phone in Robin's pocket. "I'll be behind you."

"OK." Robin was breathless and I helped her onto Faye's back.

"Hold on around her neck. Don't let go for anything. Keep your face down and your eyes closed. Go!" I slapped Faye on the backside as she took off.

Faye was running with Robin hanging on. I watched them run ahead, then I crouched down on the ground as the snow whipped sideways. I breathed deeply and shifted. I went to my lion friends, who were still dutifully waiting, and rubbed my cheek against each of theirs. I knew they could feel my immense gratitude, and they turned and left, hurrying a little in the storm.

I ran, following Faye's scent, as fast as I have ever run. The snow whirling and eddying, the wind whipping around me, I tucked my head down to cut through the wind. I was expertly dodging branches and rocks when I saw Luke's Bronco ahead, and Ethan helping Robin off Faye's back.

Luke jumped out of the car, freaking out and trying to pull Ethan away from the bear. Ethan pushed him off, picking Robin up and helping her in the car. Then I saw it. I saw Faye shift from bear to human. Luke saw it too. It was in the blink of an eye. She jumped into the backseat of the car, while Luke just stood there, frozen, staring at the spot where the bear had been.

No one had seen me, and I figured this would be a good time to shift. Luke had been through enough. I shifted easily, then ran toward the Bronco, waving my arms. Luke was still staring at nothing and took no notice. I grabbed onto his jacket and dragged him toward the car.

Ethan threw the door open. "Get in!" He yelled. "I'm driving!"

"You can drive?" I asked. It seemed a reasonable question.

"Yeah! Sure! Probably!"

I looked over at Luke. "Shouldn't you drive?" But Luke was still staring at where the bear had been. So I pushed him into the front passenger seat, and climbed into the back with Robin and Faye.

"OK, Ethan, drive!" I yelled. The Bronco began to lumber and crunch forward.

"Is everyone OK?" Ethan asked.

"I think Robin has a concussion."

"You're cut." He looked in the rear view. I looked down at my hands and noticed the cuts for the first time. I felt my forehead, and could feel bits of powdered glass and a little blood.

"It's nothing. It's from the windshield."

"If you have any cell service, call your mom. She's terrified."

I pulled my phone out of Robin's pocket. Two bars.

I texted Mom:

> We are safe. Luke has us.

It went through!

Mom immediately tried to call me but the call failed. She then texted back.

> Thank God. I love you. Come home!

"We need to get Robin to an ER right now," I said.

"That's exactly where I'm headed," Ethan said, leaning forward to see through the snow.

With a moan, Robin stirred. "I think I must have been dreaming; nothing seems real."

"Ethan, why are you driving?" Luke looked over to his left.

"Welcome back, Dad."

I leaned forward. "Are you feeling better, Luke?"

"There was a bear. Was there a bear?"

"Yes," I said, "there was a bear."

"It's a long story," Faye interjected. "Now we just have to get Robin to the doctor."

Later, at the hospital, Robin was still being looked over as I emerged from my little curtained area, sporting a bunch of small bandages all up my arms and on my forehead. I saw Ethan sitting in one of the chairs in the hallway.

I sat next to him, and he took my hand.

"You knew where to find us!" I said.

"I could sense where you were." Ethan whispered. "What happened?"

"Well, of course the weather started going crazy; it was getting really hairy and I think Dan Gann saw the avalanche coming. Get this— he just stopped the van and left us. Just ran away down the road." Ethan's jaw dropped. "The van kept rolling, like, he didn't even put it in park. While we were trying to figure out where the heck he was going, the avalanche hit us. It knocked the van over and buried us. I couldn't get out, and Robin was knocked out cold. I finally shifted to dig us out." As I was talking, my hands started to shake. I hadn't been rattled all this time, and now it was catching up to me.

"But the lions! When I started to claw my way out of the snow..." I started to tear up. "There were two lions waiting for me. They *knew* Robin was still in there. They helped me dig her out and saved us." Now the tears were running down my cheeks.

"I'm gonna end that guy." Ethan was furious. His face was turning red and I could see the veins in his neck. I had never seen him mad before, and it was intimidating.

One of the curtains pulled back from the emergency beds, and an orderly was helping Dan Gann get off the bed and into a wheelchair. He had a bandage on his head and a sling on his arm.

"Alright, Mr. Gann, you're good. Just keep the arm in the sling for a few weeks until the sprain heals. You're a lucky man." The orderly was wheeling him out to the waiting area where we were. Dan saw us sitting there and immediately looked away, like he never knew us. Ethan started to jump up and I grabbed his sleeve.

"Not here. Not yet." I calmed him. "Our time will come."

Ethan nodded, took a deep breath and put his arm around me.

13

CONCUSSED

Robin was released from the hospital with a cracked rib and a minor concussion. The doctors said it was really important to rest a while after a concussion—air travel in the first twenty-four hours was off the table—so the decision was made for Robin's dad to head back to Los Angeles, and for Robin to stay with us a few days longer. Mom was an expert at doting over the sick, so she would be in excellent hands, plied with baked goods and hearty soups. Even though I was sad she got hurt, I was elated she was going to stay with us for a while. And she was elated she was going to miss school.

Robin had been sleeping on and off since getting back from the hospital all morning, so I decided to get together with the pack and strategize a plan. We also needed Auntie Lily. The storms and strange animal behavior were ramping up, and it was only going to get worse.

I went into Robin's room to check on her. Mom was in there laying on the other twin bed. Fancy Beast was curled up next to Robin. I snapped a photo of the two of them; she'd never believe it.

"She's still sleeping?" I asked, concerned.

"Yes. She's OK though. The Doctor said she would probably sleep most of the day and be tired for the next several days. I'm keeping an eye on her." Mom was reading a book and actually sitting still for once.

"Is it OK if I go over to Ethan's house? Still no school." I looked out the window. "It's pretty calm now, though." The early afternoon light was streaming through the trees.

"Yes, that's OK. Just ask Luke to drive you home if it gets dark, OK? These freak storms are starting to really scare me; everything is just so out of whack." Mom sighed.

"Mom, do you believe in the Tuhánee legends?" I asked cautiously.

"I do." Mom sighed, deeper this time.

"Do you know how to stop it?" I knew she would know what I meant.

"I lost the ability. And I failed. So I left." Mom looked right into my eyes with so much guilt and sadness.

I walked over to her and hugged her tight. "You're never the failure Mom. Others fail you. Whatever happened, I'll bet anything I have *you* were failed."

Mom started to cry. I held on to her. She smiled weakly at me.

"You like Ethan, don't you?" She prodded, wiping away tears.

"I do." I grinned.

"He comes from good stock. Go, go see him. I'm OK. I'll keep watch over Robin til you get back. But don't be too late, alright?" Mom seemed better.

"I won't."

I went back to my room and opened my dresser drawer. Inside was the envelope I found in Sue's box, my great grandmother. I opened it, looking at the drawing of the necklace with the carved stone. I flipped it over, and again looked at the Tuhánee words; I needed to get it to Auntie Lily to translate and find out what it meant. I walked downstairs into the kitchen, where Mom always had her cell phone charging. I got into her phone—I had guessed her password a long time ago, and it was evident by now she didn't mind—there I found Auntie Lily's number and address.

I headed out the door and walked to Ethan's house. I had asked him to get the pack together. On the way I called Auntie Lily, and she agreed to meet us at Ethan's.

Walking the few miles to Ethan's house felt good. My body was sore from the accident and my muscles were achy. The exercise was loosening me up. I looked around at my sweet lake town, a home I didn't know I would love so quickly. Los Angeles was feeling farther away by the day.

The storm had everyone staying inside. The roads were quiet as they were being cleaned up by work crews. The downed trees were all over the place, and no one wanted to venture out unless they had to.

"You have the power, Anya." I heard Frederick in my mind. I stopped in my tracks and looked around. Normally I was filled with awe and wonder at these encounters, but I was suddenly stressed and overwhelmed by everything in front of me, which I had no idea how to deal with, and my awe and wonder were in short supply.

"How!!!?" I yelled to the sky. I grabbed the first thing I saw—an old beer bottle at the edge of the road—and chucked it hard at a mailbox about fifty feet away then jumped, a little embarrassed, when the bottle exploded against it.

I heard the low rumble of an engine behind me. I turned around and saw Auntie Lily's red mustang roll up next to me.

"Get in. Stop screaming at no one." Auntie Lily was smoking a Cigarillo, a big Coke sitting in the cup holder.

"Wait, you smoke?" I said, practically flabbergasted at seeing a person actually smoke in real life. Everyone in LA was so health-conscious you never saw anyone smoking.

"I do a lot of things. Let's go."

I got in the car and we peeled off down the road to Luke and Ethan's house.

The pack was all streaming into Ethan's when we arrived. Felix was carrying five boxes of pizza. "Oh good, pizza." Auntie Lily was pleased. "I hope there's no pineapple." She made a face.

"Hey." I said in a defensive tone. Why did everyone in Emerald Lake hate on the pineapple?

Inside, the fireplace was roaring and everyone was helping themselves to pizza, sans pineapple.

"Has everyone been feeling weird?" Terra asked, as they stuffed a hot slice into their mouth.

Everyone nodded in agreement. "I've been feeling really edgy." Felix admitted.

"I can't sleep." Faye added.

Auntie Lily sat down next to the fireplace with three pieces of pizza. "It's the Watanuuk. You're feeling its chaotic energy."

Ethan brought me a slice of pizza. He had added some canned pineapple rings he found in his kitchen.

"Are you for real?" I took the pizza and smiled. He shrugged and gave a sweet grin.

"Where's your dad?" I asked, looking around.

"He went on a hike. He'll probably be back soon." Ethan looked at his watch. "He's been a little weird since the other day with the bear and the avalanche and all."

"Well, he did see a bear turn into Faye."

"Yeah, we haven't talked about that yet," Ethan sighed.

I gave him a hug; I deeply understood his predicament. I certainly didn't know how to talk to Robin about all this once she was lucid.

Auntie Lily had finished her pizza, and tapped her nails on her glass to get everyone's attention.

"OK, we need a plan. The Watanuuk is coming. We all know it," she said.

"Auntie Lily, I found this." I took out the drawing of the necklace and handed it to her. "There's Tuhánee, I think, on the back. Do you know what it says?"

Jimmy rushed over to look over Auntie Lily's shoulder. He knew a little Tuhánee.

She was quiet and studied the drawing for a minute. Then she looked at the words on the back.

"It's how to capture the Watanuuk. If there is a grave upset in nature the Watanuuk will break the seal and leave its nest, creating chaos and destruction. When this happens we must rectify somehow the imbalance which stirs him awake. These are instructions to return him to the nest, sealing it back in." Auntie Lily was straining to read the words.

"Can you interpret it?" Lucy asked

"This is my mother's drawing, and her handwriting. She must have written this down from my father, Frederick. He had told me some stories about this when I was little." Auntie Lily adjusted her glasses and read the note. "It says, to reverse the unleashing:

The chosen gather together, inviting their animals to join."

Jimmy jumped in. "Make a circle..."

"Jimmy!" Auntie Lily snatched the drawing up. "I'll read it."

"Sorry, Auntie." He stepped back, but was still straining to peek.

"Ahem, as I was saying. Create a circle to represent the seal. The circle joins hands, one member facing each of the cardinal directions. The chosen asks the creator to help harness the unleashed by weakening the creature's power. The members of the circle dance clockwise while chanting:

Sha'thuun vekar Oma'shélun

No'kaar Dor'nai keluth

The stone keeper holds the sacred stone in the middle of the circle, activating its power. The Watanuuk will be attracted to the stone, but will try to destroy the keeper of it. The stone must come in contact with the Watanuuk to send it back to the nest."

"All right, we can all gather, that's easy," Jimmy said. "We can all ask our animals to join—no problem. I can draw a circle in the snow. Seems pretty simple to stand facing the cardinal directions."

"I think we have chanting down, generally. We just need to memorize the words." Ethan joined in.

Iris chimed in, "Perfect! Except we don't have the necklace or the stone. And again, who's the stone keeper? Is that one of us?" Everyone suddenly looked a little deflated.

"If it's anywhere, I bet it's in the back of Dan Gann's Souvenir shop. I saw a room behind the employee-only area that looked like it had a lot of expensive jewelry and artifacts in it." I felt like I was cracking a case wide open.

"Yeah, but he could easily have sold off some Tuhánee artifacts. Why would he keep anything? He's so greedy." Lucy pondered.

"From what I know, Dan Gann is a collector and a thief. A hoarder of precious things. If he thinks that stone has any power to it, he would keep it. He is greedy but only wants to sell cheap things for a lot of money. Not the real things." Auntie Lily added.

"Maybe any one of us is the stone keeper. Maybe it's the person who holds it?" Terra added.

"First we need to find it. Then we can worry about the keeper part. We should go break into his stupid shack and look." Jimmy suggested.

Everyone sat quietly for a minute, eating pizza and thinking.

Lucy yelled. "I can do it!" Everyone jumped, startled.

"Listen, I can shift, I'm the smallest theriotype here. As a squirrel, I can get into his shop and look for it. Easy." Lucy was excited at the possibility of a heist.

"There's a broken window you can get through." I mentioned, remembering the tape-covered window.

"Tonight, when it's dark. Lucy, I'll drive. We shouldn't all go, we have to be discreet." Felix suggested.

"OK, you and me, Felix." Lucy hopped up and down.

"And me!" Jimmy raised a hand.

"Yes, the three of us." Felix slammed a fist down on the table, sealing the plan.

"Lucy, there's a small hole in the window on the back side of the shack, covered in tape. The tape is loose; you can walk right in. It gets you into the stock room. But here's the thing. There is another door that looks like a closet, but it's a small room. That has one of those keypad entry locks on it. It was open when I was there so I was able to peek in really fast before Dan Gann caught me. That's where the glass display cases are located. Get in there and you might find what we need." I sent a picture of the necklace drawing to everyone on the Discord chat.

"Sounds like we have a plan to fix this," said Terra.

"Well, provided we get the stone. Aaaaand…" Lucy sighed.

"And?"

"If we don't stop what woke it up," said Lucy, "won't it just come back? We need a plan to stop the fracking and I don't have an idea how."

"Lucy's right," said Lily, "if the balance isn't restored, the Watanuuk won't rest."

"Oh boy," said Terra.

"Great," I said, "all we have to do is find a stone we're not even sure exists, and stop a fracking operation the whole town has been fighting for years with zero success. Easy peasy."

We all sat in silence, deflated.

"OK, we don't know how to stop the fracking," Ethan said, "but we do know how to get the Watanuuk sealed in its nest. And we think we know where the stone is. So let's do what we can do and locate the stone, and hope we come up with something about the fracking."

"Ethan's right," Auntie Lily said.

"But how do we know we'll come up with a plan for the site?" Iris asked.

"We don't," Lily said, "But no plan works without the stone, so let's focus on that for now."

"Hey Felix, now might be a good time to pull some cards." Faye suggested.

"DeerFelixKnowsAll needs to come out for a visit." Jimmy smiled proudly.

"Of course. Being a good gay, I have my man bag with all my important items, including my cards." Felix unzipped his Louis Vuitton Ave Sling bag. "Compliments of my future mother-in-law." Felix took out moisturizer, lip balm, a wallet, a charger and a velvet bag containing his favorite tarot cards.

Everyone gathered around the dining room table as Felix shuffled the deck.

"The Marseille deck is my favorite. Classic. Very popular for parlor games in the 17th and 18th century in France." Felix kept shuffling and cutting cards with great speed and flair.

"Yes, yes we know. Just throw the cards!" Jimmy snapped impatiently.

Auntie Lily looked on, intrigued. The whole pack crowded around Felix, just as the front door opened and Luke came in, sweaty from his hike. "Wow, what are you guys up to? Oh, and Auntie Lily?" Luke laughed a little at the odd gathering.

"Hi Luke." Lily waved a bony hand without looking up.

"Hey Dad, Felix is showing us Tarot," Ethan said, while barely looking up.

Luke considered all this for a moment. "Alrighty then. I'm taking a shower. This has been a super weird week." Luke muttered, headed upstairs as everyone ignored him. He stopped on the stairs and lingered a minute, as though he was going to say something. Then shook his head and continued up. "Weird week."

Felix made three piles and laid them on the table. "OK, what are we asking?"

"Maybe, will we find the necklace tonight?" Terra asked.

"OK, Terra, put the three piles into one." Terra followed Felix's instructions and picked the middle pile first, adding it to the left pile and finally adding the right pile. They handed the stack back to Felix, who with finesse selected three cards from the top of the deck. He put those aside and shuffled the deck roughly. Two cards fell out as he was shuffling. Felix grabbed the two cards and added them to the pile of three. "I have my own system. Let's see what we see." Felix turned over the cards with flair.

The first card Felix turned over was the Seven of Wands.

"Does that mean like X marks the spot?" I asked, hopeful.

"Not really. Let me see what else we have here." Felix was pensive.

The next card he turned over was the Chariot. Felix seemed encouraged by that one. Three more cards to go.

He turned over the Tower card, The Nine of Cups and lastly the The World.

"OK. All right." Felix was looking at the five cards thoughtfully.

"OK what? Explain." Iris was impatient.

"I think we're gonna get what we want here, but it's not going to be super easy. See, the seven of wands is showing obstacles, but they aren't insurmountable. The Chariot I like next to the Seven of Wands, because if we stay focused, we will overcome any problems to victory. The Tower, well now that can be a little chaotic, shaking things up. It looks bad, it could be bad, but it also signifies moments of growth and a chance for a new start."

"Oh God, I hate moments of growth. That is just a way to say everything is awful." Iris moaned, slamming her head on the table.

"Everyone hates moments of growth. But we do it." Auntie Lily added.

"Iris, But, but... wait, we have the Nine of Cups which is great! That's a wish coming true. And look, look at the World card. You can't do any better than the World card. That makes me think we got this in the bag." Felix slammed his hands down on the cards. "Guys, we're gonna be victorious."

Felix gathered his cards and put them back in his little velvet pouch.

"Tonight. We are the champions. My friends."

"Let me guess. We'll keep fighting, til the end?" Jimmy teased.

"No time for losers, Jimmy." Felix grabbed Jimmy and hugged him tight.

"Alright Queen. Let's go." Jimmy was pulling Felix out the door. "I need a day nap."

"Anya, I will drive you home." Auntie Lily was ready to go at the door with her purse in hand.

I looked at Ethan, smiling. "Thank you for my pineapple." I kissed him goodbye. "We'll talk later. I'm going to check on Robin."

"Of course. Let me know how she's feeling." Ethan glowed.

"I wanna go tonight." I whispered.

"We're going." Ethan grinned mischievously.

"Hurry up Anya, I'm too old to wait." Auntie Lily wasn't mad, just direct.

"Coming!" I winked at Ethan and scooted out the door.

Once home I ran upstairs to check on Robin. She was propped up in bed, snacking on some grapes. "You're awake!" I shouted, happily.

"Sorta." Robin looked tired and groggy. "They gave me those pain pills for my ribs. I feel NO pain! But I am LOOPY!" Robin was laughing and then holding her side. "Oh, OK, some pain."

"Girl, don't laugh. Shhhh, shhhhh" I soothed.

"I can tell ya though, your mom is the best nurse. I think she's downstairs making pies or something. I kinda wanna be hurt for like a month here." Robin had grapes stuffed in her cheeks like a chipmunk.

"I gotta show you something." I took out my phone and showed Robin the photo of Fancy Beast sleeping with her.

Robin's eyes got huge. "NO!"

"Oh yes. See?" I laughed.

"That's AI." Robin refused to believe it.

"It's not! Mom was here, she can attest to the fact that Fancy Beast does indeed, care for you." I pointed the photo directly at Robin.

"I'll consider it." Robin leaned back, gently stretching. "Anya, I think I hallucinated. What happened?"

I carefully considered what I'd say next.

"What do you remember?" I asked cautiously.

"A bad lake tour. A storm that seemed to come out of nowhere. Here's where it gets fuzzy. I remember we got hit by something." Robin was thinking.

"That was the avalanche." I confirmed.

"OK, yeah. But then you were gone. And I think a mountain lion was trying to kill me, but in the van, that was buried? It didn't make any sense." Robin was struggling to remember.

"What do you think happened then?" I questioned, sitting on the bed with Robin.

"I saw you. Then you told me to ride a bear?" Robin started laughing and wincing at the same time. "That can't be correct. That's where I'm crazy, right? Those are the pills talking." Robin was suddenly serious, looking at me closely, holding her side.

"That is so crazy. Yeah, crazy." I laughed weirdly. "But..." I put my face in my hands and squashed my face, rubbing my eyes as though this would help somehow. Robin went very quiet; I could feel her eyes on me. I pulled my face down into a basset-hound mug, trying not to look at her. I gave up and looked at her.

"But what?" Robin was oddly not loud when she said that.

I stood up and walked around in tight circles trying to figure out how to explain everything. "Apparently, well.. you know how I like cats? And P-22," I started.

"Yeah. Cats. OK. P-22." Robin was trying to follow me.

"OK, well... hmmm. So my new friend group, they are therians." I guess I'd start there.

"Therians, OK. Like animal fans. Wearing tails? I think I've seen this on TikTok or something." Robin was gamely trying to keep up.

"Sorta. So, I guess the short version is we can all shape-shift into animals and communicate with other animals and the balance of nature and humans is at stake and there's a Tuhánee legendary lake monster that is probably gonna explode out of the lake at any time and kill and destroy things and we kinda have to stop it." I spit it all out.

"And what's the long version of this story?" Robin seemed concerned.

"You rode a bear. It was Faye. The mountain lion, that was me, dragging you out of the van. It was the only way I could dig us out." I looked at Robin dead serious.

Robin narrowed her eyes, looking at me suspiciously, waiting for me to start laughing. When I didn't she pulled back a little in her body language. I could smell a little fear.

"You're scared." I said.

"Uhh, well, yeah." Robin seemed uneasy.

"I can smell it on you." I said.

"Rude."

I sat on the bed again. "I know this sounds insane. It is insane. But somehow, it's true." I felt relief telling her, even if she thought I was nuts.

I could hear Mom coming up the stairs, humming. She whisked into the room. "Oh Anya, I didn't even know you were back." She kissed me on the head and took Robin's empty bowl.

We both sat there silently.

"Girls? Everything all right?" Mom looked at us, confused.

"Yeah, I'm just feeling sleepy. I think I'll take a nap." Robin scooted down in the bed and pulled the covers up to her chin.

"I'm actually super tired too. I might take a nap in my room." I got up and started through the closet passageway to my room.

"OK. I'll go downstairs and try and be quiet so you two can rest. Call me if you need anything." Mom left the room closing the door.

I went into my bedroom and sat on the bed. That did not go well. I didn't know if Robin thought I was lying, or if she was just weirded out because it was all true. I looked down at my ring, the sapphire glowing. I really was tired. I laid back on my bed looking at the ceiling, thinking about it all. My eyes shut. The buzzing began and I was hurling through the great unknown. I landed in the familiar library. The statues of the mountain lions were gone, but two live lions were lounging in front of the fireplace, relaxing. My eyes adjusted to the room and lighting. Frederick was sitting in a big chair, wearing his tuxedo.

"You're my great grandfather?" I smiled, looking at the ring on my finger.

"That I am. You're going to wake up in a minute, but show your friend. You need to show her." Frederick pointed to the lounging lions.

And in a flash I was back in my body. I sat up looking outside at the calm weather, grateful no freak storms were brewing. I stood up, stretching my sore body, moving from side to side. I snuck through the closet passageway and peeked in at Robin. She was asleep, but restless. I thought about what Frederick said. Show her. I walked into her room and sat on her bed. "Robin." I whispered gently rocking her. Robin stirred slightly. "Robin, wake up." I whispered louder.

"What? What's wrong?" Robin opened her eyes groggily.

"I need to show you something." I said nervously.

"OK." Robin sat up slowly. "I have to pee."

"Oh OK, come on, I'll help you." I carefully and slowly helped Robin out of bed. She breathed deeply, holding her side and whining. "I think I need another pain pill." She groaned.

"OK, after the bathroom and what I need to show you." I urged.

I walked Robin through the actual door to my room to use the bathroom. Crouching through the passageway would be too painful for her. She went into the bathroom and I sat back on my bed, waiting for her and wondering when was a good time to shift. I got up, shut the door and paced my room for a minute. "Are you OK?" I called into her.

"Yeah, I'm OK. I'll be out in a minute. I'm slow." Robin seemed guarded and Robin was never guarded.

Now or never, I thought. I sat on my bed and breathed in deeply. I connected to my mountain lions and saw us as one. And just like that, I was in lion form. It was weird being in my room like this. Fancy Beast shot out from under the bed and flew into the closet, out into Robin's room, and down the stairs. God, I should have checked under the bed. Poor thing.

I jumped up onto my bed and laid down, trying to look casual. I heard the toilet flush, and for a split second I considered shifting back.

Robin opened the door and stood in the doorway, just staring at me. Frozen.

I tried to think how to act. Maybe I could strike a submissive pose, so she wouldn't feel threatened? I rolled over on my back, exposing my belly like a friendly dog.

"Ohhhh, ahhhhhh, wow." Robin slowly shuffled over to the bed where I was laying down.

"Uhh, OK. I assume you can't speak to me." Robin was curious, yet rightfully wigged out. I could not speak. I could try and connect, to see if I could communicate with her in her mind. I tried, but nothing was transmitting to her.

Robin stood looking at me. I sat up and she jumped back quickly. "Ohhh, oww." She held her side. Fancy Beast peeked out from behind the closet door. *It's OK, it's me*, I said. She relaxed a little but stayed behind the door.

I put my head down low, still on the bed. Robin came closer again and reached a hand out cautiously. She pet my head for a minute. "OK, this is too weird. Can you go back to Anya please?" Robin looked out the window and on the railing was a huge eagle. Ethan. "Let me guess, that's your boyfriend, right?" Robin wasn't really mad but was sounding mad. "OK, I'm going to my room, I'm taking a pain pill and maybe you can become my best friend again and not a giant mountain lion?" Robin shook her head in disbelief and walked out the door into the hallway.

I breathed deeply and instantly shifted back into my human form. Fancy Beast zoomed away again. Well that was awkward. I looked out the window. Ethan was standing by the door, waiting for me to let him in.

"That didn't seem to go over as well as maybe you thought?" Ethan creeped in my room slowly.

"Yeah, I think she is just processing. And she's also on a lot of pain meds." I said, hopeful. "Let's give her a minute."

"Are you all right?" Ethan hugged me close.

"I don't know. I mean, who can advise a person on this? Oh, my best friend is being weird 'cause I turned into a mountain lion in front of her. There's no user guide on this." I sighed epically.

"I got nothing, Anya. I'm avoiding my dad because he saw Faye turn into a bear and now he's just freaking out silently and dealing with it by exercising excessively." We sighed together.

"Well, tonight we can hang back and watch how it goes at Dan Gann's. They may need backup. If nothing else, I'm not entirely sure how Lucy in squirrel form is gonna open a door." Ethan started busting up. The whole situation was absurd.

"You can stay for dinner, I'm sure Mom is making some food."

"Wait. Your mom is making food?"

"Oh shut up. Let's check on Robin." I went the traditional route, and walked through the main door instead of the closet. I poked my head in and Robin was sitting up in bed, staring out the window. It was lightly snowing.

"Can we come in?" I asked quietly.

"Of course." Robin scooted up a little more so she was sitting higher up. I walked in and Ethan came in behind me.

"Hi Robin. How ya feeling?" Ethan smiled like the cheshire cat.

"Well everything kinda hurts. Including my feelings." Robin looked sad. I rushed over to her. "I am so sorry. I never, ever meant to make you feel bad." I was overwhelmed and starting to cry.

"No, no. Anya, don't shame-spiral. It's not your fault. I'm not mad. I just feel left out you didn't tell me this sooner." I could tell Robin knew I was on the verge of a full-on meltdown, and she was doing her best to mitigate it.

But I couldn't stop crying. I felt so terrible I hurt Robin and I didn't know how to process any of it. I hated myself. I felt so selfish. Ethan tried to help. "Anya, it's not one of those areas where there's a known way to handle it, right?" He looked to Robin for backup. I was on the floor, inconsolable.

"That's right, Ethan. Normally, normally, when people shift into animals and ask non-shifting people to ride wild animals out of a blizzard, the protocol is..." Robin's face crumpled and she began cracking up. Ethan started laughing too. I was lost in my shame, but far away I could hear them both laughing. Instantly I found it impossible to be sad, and my tears changed to tears of laughter.

14

———

JENNY JENNY

Mom made an incredible feast, and in spite of the earlier weirdness, Robin seemed to be a little more like herself. We joked and talked and overall had a really fun meal. Ethan and I helped Robin back upstairs, where she took her medicine and hit the bed early.

Before I shut the door to her room she called me over. "Anya," Robin looked so sleepy. "This has been a super strange few days. I don't totally understand what's going on, but maybe when I'm less concussed and medicated, you can tell me everything."

"I will tell you everything." I promised.

I shut the door softly and went back into my room. Ethan was sitting on my bed looking out the window at the snow falling.

"It's almost time to go," he said, looking excited. I sat next to Ethan and leaned my whole body against him. He put his arm around me and leaned back. "I'll say goodnight to Mom and sneak out and meet you there."

Ethan ran his hands through my hair and we just sat there for a few minutes. Finally, he stood up and opened the door to the deck. "Time to go, I'll see you soon." He ran back over to me and kissed me really slow and gently. My whole body shook.

"You make me happy." He smiled. Then he headed out the door. And just like that, he was in flight, on his way to the souvenir shack.

I heard Mom coming up the stairs. She was checking in on Robin. "Mom?" I whispered, peeking out the bedroom door.

Mom tiptoed back from Robin's room. "She's asleep. She needs rest. Where's Ethan?"

"He just left out the back door. I'm going to bed early too. I'm still sore from the accident." I said, which was half true.

"OK, honey. I'm going to work on some baskets for Auntie Lily. Sleep well." Mom kissed me on the cheek and headed downstairs. I shut the door. Fancy Beast was under the bed, still a little spooked from earlier. I made sure the closet doors were open to Robin's room so she could go sleep with her. I turned out the lights and quietly opened the door. The snow was falling gently. I breathed in deeply, picturing my mountain lions, and instantly shifted.

Once shifted, I could sense Ethan. He was already at the souvenir shack, waiting for me. I made my way to him, running through the back yards and staying out of sight. With my keen predatory skills I could run fast and silently over the snow, undetected. I slinked around the back area of the souvenir shack and crouched behind the dumpsters, where I shifted back to Anya form. Ethan was up on one of the bear totems, surveying the landscape. He flew down by the dumpsters and shifted back.

"Hi. So, Felix's car just parked down the street."

I hugged Ethan. "Hi. Great, they should be here in a minute."

There was one streetlight in front of the souvenir shop which cast the building and parking lot in an ominous light. It wasn't a busy area this time of night, and with the storms it was more deserted than usual. That weird cold fog was settling in again.

Jimmy, Lucy and Felix slowly materialized out of the fog. "Hey, guys!" Ethan whispered loudly, waving, getting their attention.

"What are you two doing here?" Jimmy was surprised to see us.

"Like we would sit this one out," I said.

"It's a perfect night for this; it's like a ghost town right now. And with the fog, no one is going to see us." Lucy said, looking around pleased.

"He doesn't have a security system, does he?" Ethan asked scanning the roofline of the shop for cameras.

"No. I was in there. All he has is that keypad lock on the door inside the employee area," I said confidently.

"Are you ready, Lucy?" I asked, excited.

"I am so ready." Lucy slipped into the trees. She came running back out in squirrel form, and scurried up the side of the shop. She poked her head into the tape flap covering the broken window. Ethan, Felix and I hung back over by the dumpsters in the shadows, staying out of sight.

Lucy was in. Jimmy was glued to the side of the building by the broken window, keeping an eye on Lucy. Once inside, Lucy shifted back to human form. She opened the back door to the employee area for us to come inside. We quickly snuck in.

"It smells gross in here. And what a pig Dan is, look at this place." Lucy complained, looking at the dusty array of back stock. There were filthy boxes everywhere and shelves lined with all kinds of strange, random items. Nothing looked to have been cleaned in years.

"Let's just get into the room and get out of here." Felix said nervously.

"Crap, the door is locked. It was left open the other day." I rattled the knob, but it wouldn't budge.

"I wonder if there's any other way into the room." Jimmy was looking around for cracks or anyplace that Lucy could maybe crawl into.

"It's locked up tight." Lucy sighed, defeated.

"We could try and guess a code." Ethan suggested.

"There is literally like a 1 in 3 million chance we could guess it, even if we knew the number of digits. Not to mention if we get it wrong multiple times, which we will, it will probably lock us out of the system altogether." I was pacing back and forth, frustrated.

We all heard a car pull into the parking lot. The headlights lit up the whole area as the tires creaked on the snow.

"Get out, get out!" Jimmy panicked.

"I'm shifting and staying inside. You guys go, quick." Lucy was pushing us out the back door, as we heard the car door slam. Ethan, Felix, Jimmy and I ran quietly across the lot and hid behind the dumpsters. My heart was beating out of my chest. After a moment, I carefully peeked around the building and saw a beat-up Toyota truck.

It appeared Russell hadn't quit his job at the souvenir shop yet; he exited the Toyota holding a box and a briefcase, trying to steady both as he navigated the slippery snow. He opened the front door to the shop and locked it behind him, the discordant bells clanging.

"Guys, that's Russell. He works here, and from what I know, isn't a Dan fan. I don't know why he's here this late. Come with me," I said, *"very quietly."* I crouched down and trotted across the lot to the back wall of the store, Ethan, Jimmy, and Felix following behind. I squatted down, my back to the wall, and the others followed suit.

A door opened loudly inside. Russell was entering the back area. I pointed upward, indicating I was going to take a look through the window above us, then I inched up, took a quick glance, then ducked back down. He was there, fortunately turned toward the door to the back room, so I eased back up, holding my breath, and watched.

Russell threw the box and the briefcase down, swearing and irritated. He stood in front of the door to the back room, staring at the code pad, blankly for a moment. He cracked his neck, squinting his eyes shut. He started singing to himself, surprisingly loudly and a little off-key.

"JENNY, DON'T CHANGE YOUR NUMBER," he brayed.

Felix started frantically tapping my leg, making me almost jump out of my skin. I looked down at him, annoyed, while he gestured excitedly at me to come down. I squatted next to him, scowling.

"*I know the code!*" He whispered in my ear. "I know it! It's an 80's song." Felix was trying to be quiet but as he continued he got louder.

Jimmy made a violent *SHHHHH* gesture, looking at Felix.

"Sorry." Felix mouthed.

I crept back up to the window. "I GOT IT, I GOOOOOT IT, I GOT IT," Russell wailed. I saw Lucy peek her little head above one of the boxes. "I GOT YOUR NUMBER ON THE WALL..."

The door popped open, and Russell kicked the box inside with his foot and threw the briefcase in after it, not even bothering to enter the room. Russell got on his phone. He was making a call while shutting the door; I could hear the door lock automatically a second after.

"Yes Dan, they're in the antique room. Exactly where you asked me to put them. Yes... Yes... OK." Russell hung up, irritated. "A-hole," he snarled. He headed back toward the main door, and a few seconds later, we heard the Toyota start up and drive away

Everyone let out a breath.

"Well, that was nauseating," Lucy said as she opened the back door to let us back inside. "Hurry up." She waved us in.

We all hustled inside, looking around suspiciously, rattled. "OK, what's the code, Felix?" Jimmy looked wide-eyed and excited as he stood in front of the keypad.

"Eight six seven five three oh ni-eeeiune," He sang, delighted. *"Jenny. Jenny, who can I turn to? You give me something I can hold on to!"* Felix sang, and did a little '80s dance.

"Wait, wait, don't sing the whole song. Slower. Do the code again, I don't remember this song." Jimmy said.

"What?! It's Tommy Tutone. A one hit wonder! It was released in 1981 and hit number 4 on the Billboard top 100 and number 1 on.."

"FELIX!!! Seriously man, stop. What is the dang number?! Impress me with your '80s rock knowledge once we're out of here!"

"Sorry. 8... 6... 7..." He was still singing a little.

Jimmy was punching in the numbers carefully.

"5... 3... 0... 9," Felix trailed off, humming.

The door opened.

"Oh my God Felix, you're amazing." I beamed, impressed.

"We are in!" Lucy announced. We all jammed into the back room, investigating the surroundings. Inside the small room were actual vintage Tuhánee baskets, in pristine condition; that looked very old. They were lined up on a shelf above the glass display cases. Inside the cases were all sorts of different rings and precious stones. Small sculptures and beaded jewelry lined the cases.

"Do you see the stone?" Felix asked.

"Not yet." Lucy was scanning the tops of the glass cases looking at each item carefully. I was also looking at cases on the other side of the room. I saw there was a small velvet box in the corner of one of the cases.

"What do we have here?" I said quietly to myself, as I carefully slid the back of the glass case door to the side and grabbed the box. It was an old jewelry box that had tight, rusted hinges. It took a little effort to open it and once I did it snapped opened abruptly.

BINGO! The beaded necklace and yellow stone flew out, landing on the floor.

"You found it!" Jimmy yelled.

I carefully picked up the reddish orange stone and looked at it. It was bigger than I imagined from the drawings, and fit neatly in the palm of my hand. It was a flawless golden carnelian, and the Tuhánee eagle engraved on the front was obviously the one from the drawing. We all gathered around the stone and just stared at it, waiting for it to do some freaky magical voodoo all by itself.

"I don't think it's going to do anything." Jimmy chuckled.

"I mean weird stuff has been happening left and right, you never know!" Lucy pointed out.

I tucked it back into the beaded pouch necklace, shutting the velvet box. It thudded loudly, almost pinching my fingers.

"Let's get out of here." Felix said.

"Wait, I'm gonna look in the box Russell brought. I'm curious." Ethan rubbed his hands together, excited.

"We really should just get out now." I said. "Come on." Lucy, Jimmy and Felix were out the backdoor.

Ethan squatted over the box on the floor and unfolded the top flaps. Inside was stacked rows of cash bundled in Star Light Casino currency bands. "What?!" Ethan exclaimed. He pulled a thick stack out, turning it over, looking at it.

"Oh my God, put it back Ethan." I was nervous.

Jimmy yelled through the window. "Someone is coming! A car!"

"Anya, go!" Ethan urged as he was trying to get the money back into the box. I ran out the back door and Jimmy shut it behind me.

"Wait, Ethan!" I tugged on Jimmy, who grabbed me and threw me to the ground, holding his finger over his mouth. "Shhhhhh! No time."

The bells jingled from the front door opening. Jimmy and I remained silent, laying in the snow next to the shack. Ethan was still inside.

I couldn't help myself and wiggled away from Jimmy to look in the window. The door to the back room was open. The employee-room door flew open and Dan Gann marched in, arm still in a sling.

"Stupid kid can't close a door!" Dan was furious and stomped into the antique room.

I looked up and saw Ethan in eagle form, perched on a high shelf, standing absolutely still. He was stuck between a taxidermy badger and a large vase. Dan came out of the antique room carrying the box of money with one arm and balancing the brief case on top of it. He kicked the door closed so hard the shop shook. Dan barged through the front door, jangling the bells. I could hear him on the phone yelling at Russell. "How hard is it to close a door, son!" Dan's voice echoed against the fog and vacant street. "No, No! You didn't!" The car door slammed shut and Dan sped away, kicking up snow as his car pulled out of the lot.

I slid down the side of the shop with my hands over my face, completely relieved.

Ethan came out of the door, holding his chest. "That was terrifying." He laughed.

"Dude. Dude." Felix shook his head. "That was close."

I ran up and shoved Ethan. "Oh my God, that was brilliant!" I looked to the others. "You should have seen him!"

"Where did you hide?" Lucy asked.

Ethan shrugged, grinning. "He shifted to eagle and got on the shelf next to the stuffed badger!" I said.

"Stop!!" Lucy was laughing.

"He just sat there staring at Dan. The guy didn't even notice!!"

We all walked back to Felix's car, laughing. The fog was so thick we could barely see two feet in front of us. Once in the car, I held up the stone and we all admired it, savoring our victory.

"Guys, that was some serious heist action." Felix was pumped. He started cueing some music. "I have just the thing. Our victory song." He cranked the volume.

We spun out of the lot, "867-5309" blasting from the stereo.

Ethan and I silently snuck back into my room from the back stairs. All was quiet and we fell onto the bed, exhausted.

"That was exciting." I said, looking over at Ethan who looked asleep already. "Ethan?" I shook him lightly. He didn't open his eyes or move. "Ethan!" I was louder, but still in a hushed tone so I didn't wake up Robin or Mom. Ethan was motionless. "Ethan!" I poked him. Nothing. I propped myself up on my arm, looking directly into his face, super close. I started breathing heavily, right into his nose. Finally he cracked and exploded with laughter.

"Shhhhh! You're going to wake everyone up!" I slapped my hand over his mouth. He shook uncontrollably. I couldn't hold it in any longer and started laughing too. The more we tried to contain it, the less we could.

"And what kind of illegal shenanigans are going on here?" Robin was standing in the closet door, her hair going in all directions, wearing fuzzy rabbit slippers and holding Fancy Beast under her arm.

"Oh my God Fancy Beast is letting you hold her!?" I was shocked.

"Yes, we are besties now." Robin dropped Fancy Beast at her feet. The beast attacked the rabbit slippers as Robin hopped up and down, trying to escape the kill fury of The Beast. Robin jumped into the bed with us for refuge.

"Sorry we woke you." Ethan said.

"It's OK. All I've been doing is sleeping." Robin rubbed her eyes. "I'm getting under the covers. Move over bird and cat." She slid under the covers between us. I lit the pine candle. "Ambiance." I declared. Fancy Beast jumped up, calmer, and started making muffins on me.

The three of us just quietly stared at the ceiling, while the candlelight danced around, creating interesting shadows. It was hypnotic. Ethan yawned. I yawned. And within moments we were all asleep.

I heard a strange sound, almost like a slapping noise. It stirred me awake and I opened my eyes. I looked around the room, trying to figure out where the noise was coming from. The clock read 2:40AM. Ethan roused, turning on his side, still mostly asleep. Robin was snoring. Fancy Beast was wide awake, her eyes locked on the windows. I rubbed my face and looked at what had caught her attention.

There was a vast, loud murmur, like a rustling, which seemed to come from every direction, punctuated by an occasional *THUD*. It sounded like a hailstorm was starting. *WHACK!* Something had definitely hit one of the windows. Sideways hail? I sat up and strained to see out the windows. The blackness outside seemed to be moving.

I slowly inched out of bed and approached the windows. The night sky seemed to be a tornado of dark leaves, violently swirling. I wondered if this was one of my dreams. But it was all wrong for that. On one of the windows there was a large dark streak, and I came closer, almost afraid of what I'd see. I touched the cold glass, squinting at the stain, which I now saw had a distinct burgundy color. The cold seemed to travel up my fingers and through my whole body, standing my hair on end.

It was blood.

THWACK!! Something hit the window directly next to my face. I must have screamed.

Ethan sat up suddenly. "What's wrong!?"

Robin was also waking up. "Guys, what is it?"

I looked on the deck at what had hit the window. It lay twitching, dying.

A bat.

I looked again at the sky. The fluttering tornado was all bats, swarming, hundreds of thousands of them. They were everywhere. They were smashing into the streetlights, the boathouse, our cabin, my window, anything and everything.

Robin and Ethan came to the window. I whispered, "Bats." We stared out the window, awestruck. WHACK!! Another bat hit the glass, cracking it slightly.

"Should we get away from the windows?" Ethan asked. We stayed at the window, mesmerized.

"Look," I said. The mass of bats started thinning out; the sliver of moon they had blotted out was now visible. Across the lake, we could see the bats expanding into a vast circle, like a hurricane, its empty eye centered on the lake. Now we were drawn inside the eye as it grew, and we could see it must be at least a mile wide. The immense, circular cloud of bats shimmered in the dim moonlight, and we could see the sky, full of brilliant stars.

Suddenly, the slim crescent of the moon winked out, as though someone had turned off a switch. The stars around it began to disappear and reappear. A gigantic shadow was moving across the sky.

"Anya??" Ethan croaked.

I turned to them. "Its coming."

15

THE RITUAL

"Felix, get Jimmy, get everyone. Meet us Anya's house—now." Ethan hung up the phone. "They're already in the car on their way."

"What are we gonna do?" I looked at Ethan, confused.

"I've been thinking; we need to get to the fracking site. The animals can hear us, the way we can sense each other. We need to communicate to them and to the Watanuuk to go to that location. I'm hoping if we tap into the Watanuuk it will follow the signal. Once its there, well, I don't know that part, but I'm hoping it demolishes the whole place. We do the ritual, and if everything goes perfectly we get it back in the nest." Ethan shrugged.

"Yeah, it doesn't look like the bats are on a wavelength with the Watanuuk. Can you feel it? How upset they are?" I asked.

"Yeah," Ethan looked grim. "I can feel it."

"OK, listen," I said. "We know the stone will draw the Watanuuk to its holder. The keeper of the stone gives the stone its power. So it'll try to destroy whoever is holding it, without touching it."

"And the holder will try to touch the Watanuuk with the stone without getting destroyed," Ethan added.

"Yes," I replied.

"OK, I see where you're going with this." Ethan did not look pleased about where I was going with this.

"Sorry."

"No, you're right."

"Guys, this all sounds insane," Robin said. "What are you talking about?"

"So basically," Ethan said, sighing, "I'm gonna have to flap around like a fool with this dumb stone and let the Watanuuk try to kill me. I'll get it chasing the stone all through the fracking site, where it will destroy everything except me, or so we hope. And then I'll hit it with the stone, without letting it hit me first, because then I will also die. Easy, right?"

"Oh," Robin said. "That's not good." We stood there in silence a moment.

"I for one am not super excited about this!" Ethan said, staring out at the lake.

"Is there a better plan?" I said. We sat in silence another moment.

"Nope, that's the plan. Robin, grab a jacket, you're coming with us." Ethan ordered.

We began to throw on our snow clothes. My phone buzzed. "Auntie Lily is up. She just texted me."

"Do you think it's about the bats?" Ethan said facetiously, as bats continued to smash against the house. "It's probably about the bats! It could be something else at three in the morning, what do you think?!"

"Bats." I held up my phone so they could read the text:

> Its coming.

Ethan's phone buzzed. "Oh, look, it's my dad." He glanced at his phone. "Think he wants me to take out the trash?"

"What?"

"Nope, it's about the bats. We better get a move on."

"What do I do?!" Robin was panicked and standing by the closet, wearing a big jacket and fuzzy hat, her pajamas still on. "I don't have magical animal shifty powers like you guys."

"Just come with us." I grabbed Robin's hand.

"OK, OK." She was dazed.

I grabbed the stone and placed it in my jacket pocket. "Are you ready?" I said to Ethan.

"I'm ready." He looked at me with confidence.

Mom had run up the stairs, hearing the commotion. She was standing in the doorway, her eyes wide.

"Anya!?" She was half awake, and frightened. "What's going on?" I pointed out the window; she stepped over to it, slack-jawed.

"My God, its coming."

A horn was honking outside. I ran over to Mom and hugged her. "I love you. We have to go. We have to do the ritual and get the Watanuuk back into the nest."

Mom looked at me. "You can't do the ritual, you don't have the stone."

"We have it. We're going to the fracking site." There was no time to explain any more. The three of us ran down the stairs and out the front door.

Felix was shouting for us to get in. The bats were everywhere, thousands of them, flying erratically.

"Keep your heads down!" Ethan shouted. The bats were smacking into us and hitting Felix's car. Some were dying, some were just stunned, but all of them completely haywire and incapable of navigating.

We all crammed into the car.

"You know where to go Felix?" Terra asked.

"Yeah, I told him where to go," Jimmy said.

"Move, move, move!" Iris yelled from the back.

We drove off as quickly as we could, the headlights shining against the dark brown flurry of the swarm of bats. We could barely see where we were going, and Felix leaned forward, straining to make out the road. If it hadn't been for the snow I doubt we could have seen anything. We felt awful, the bats' confusion and misery seeping into our animal senses, and whenever one splatted against the car, our hearts ached.

"You're doing great, Felix," I said.

"This is certainly the best batnado driving I've ever experienced. Five stars," Ethan said. Felix gave a tense chuckle.

"Guys, try something. Everyone send thoughts out to your theriotypes to meet us at the fracking site. Tell them we need all the help we can get. Maybe they will sense it and show up," Jimmy suggested. "I don't know what they can do, but maybe they can help trash the equipment."

The fog of bats was thinning out, and I could see the lights from the construction cranes shining in the distance. We were almost there. The car was silent as we all focused on our animal friends. Before long, we could see the high fence of the site, and the entry gate, down at the end of the road.

Felix suddenly darted off onto a little fire road, basically a dirt track through the woods, and we were now closely surrounded by tall trees, headed up a steep hill. It was very dark, save for the light from the headlights, and in the distance I saw a pair of eyes, shining in the light, and then another. Soon, as we turned around switchbacks, climbing the hill, wherever the lights touched the woods, dozens of reflective eyes glowed back at us. It had worked. They were here.

There was a sense of calm coming over us; we all knew what we had to do, and we didn't have the luxury of time to panic.

We parked in a clearing on the top of the hill and got out; the clearing extended down the side of the hill all the way to the site, and we had a clear view. Throngs of deer, wolves, bears, coyotes, raccoons, squirrels, lions, skunks, and beavers gathered at the edge of the clearing, watching us.

Below, in the lights of the fracking compound, we could see some of the night crew milling around. They seemed to have stopped doing whatever they normally do, and were just looking at all the bats and animals massing around the site.

I could see a tall Sprinter-type van in the compound, with a tacky wrap that looked very much like the one on the van we almost died in.

I squinted. "Is that the Dan Gann van?"

Robin raised an eyebrow. "The Dan Gann van got crushed like a soda can. Remember?"

I was not going to be outdone. "The man can have more than one van. It appears to be a Dodge Ram. It's all part of the plan."

"Oh my God, will you two shut up!" Jimmy sputtered. "We have a ritual to perform!"

Then the ground started shaking violently. One of the cranes lurched sickeningly from side to side, but stayed upright. The trees swayed and rustled.

"Oh God, is that another quake!?" Robin yelled.

"I think that's the Watanuuk, Robin." Jimmy looked back at us, his eyes huge.

Jimmy was running around a flat portion of the clearing, looking for a stick. "I'm going to get the circle drawn out for the ritual."

I focused on sending the Watanuuk energy. I was doing anything I could think of to lure him to us. I took the necklace out of my pocket and got the stone out. It was smooth and warm in my hand. I looked at the carved eagle on it and rubbed it between my palms. It began to light up.

"Guys, look!" I held the stone in my palm. The glowing was faint, but seemed to be pulsing and getting brighter.

"Whoa, how did you do that?" Robin asked, mystified.

"I didn't really do anything, I just took it out." I could feel it warming my hand.

It seemed suddenly quieter. The stars shimmered in the cold sky.

"I think it's getting closer." Terra said quietly.

"Hear that?" I said.

"Hear what?" Robin looked around nervously.

"Exactly. The bats are gone."

Everyone took this in and started scanning the sky, but we could see nothing but the cold starlight and the sliver of moon.

Jimmy had made the circle, and placed a pinecone at one end of it. "OK, north." He went around it, placing the other pinecones. "South. East. West."

"How do you know exactly where true north is?" Robin asked.

The rest of us looked at the circle. "No, that's right," I said.

Robin turned to me. "Wait, how do *you* know? You used to get lost at the mall."

"Pack, close your eyes," I said. They stood straight and closed their eyes. "Face south-southeast!" We whirled as one, facing the same direction. "Back to north!" We whipped around, opening our eyes, lined up perfectly with the northern pinecone.

"It's an animal thing," Faye said.

Robin shook her head. "Of course it is."

Suddenly we heard a metallic groaning emanating from the bottom of the hill. A huge mass of animals had gathered there, and were pressing against the chain-link fence with so much force it was beginning to buckle; we could hear links snapping and the moaning of the posts bending. The concertina wire on the top of the fence *sproinged* around crazily, like some kind of deadly Slinky. The handful of workers were strung out along the fence line, trying to stop the herds of animals coming in, but even from this distance we could see they were not so sure about this plan.

Toward the center of the compound, I could see a man standing on the steps of an office trailer; he was looking out at the fence line with a pair of binoculars. I saw he had on a loud plaid sport coat. Dan himself. He took the binoculars away from his eyes and looked around worriedly.

Then, all at once, the fence gave way all along its length, sections of link bursting with a roar, the fence posts bending every which way like paperclips. The workers abandoned whatever plan they had made, and ran for it.

"Oh wow!" Lucy yelled.

Our sudden joy at part of our plan working was short-lived; we could all feel the nauseous aura of what was to come. I looked down, trying not to throw up. The stone in my hand was getting brighter.

"Everyone! Get in place around the circle!" Jimmy yelled.

"What do I do!?!" Robin cried.

"Get inside the car. Stay in the car!" I told her. She jumped into the front seat, locking the doors.

"We have to start the ritual!" Jimmy yelled, frantically.

I got in the middle, holding the stone. Everyone else took their places around the circle.

"Everyone focus! FOCUS! We ask the elements of Earth, air, fire and water to come to our aid and join us. We need your strength to harness the unleashed! Please come to us. Earth, air, fire and water! Earth, air, fire and water!"

We all joined in. "Earth, air, fire and water!"

Robin looked on, wide-eyed; she was yelling in the car, "Earth, air, fire and water!" She was so loud. We all looked back at the car, a few of us giving her a thumbs up. The earth began to rumble.

The night crew were all racing around the site wildly, pointing and yelling at the animals that were charging in. Bears were knocking over trash cans, mountain lions were rushing towards the office trailer. A few of the workers climbed up on the trucks and cranes to get above the animals. On top of this, a wild wind came out of nowhere in the calm night, blowing debris across the site, branches flying off the trees.

"Earth, air, fire, water!" We chanted. The clear sky exploded with lightning, followed by the loudest thunderclap I have ever heard. As the lightning lit up the sky, I thought I saw a huge black shadow coming over the ridge from the direction of the lake.

"Ethan, did you see that!?" I screamed, pointing at the ridge.

"No, what, what did you see?" He was straining to see anything in this pitch dark. Even his eagle sight was not clocking anything. The ground shook harder than ever, and suddenly the wind began to blow fiercely. We were struggling to stay standing.

Just then, the clearing was flooded with bright white lights, and Auntie's red Mustang came to a screeching halt. Mom and Auntie Lily jumped out of the car.

Rain began to fall from nowhere; the sky remained crystal clear, the stars shimmering through the drops. Jimmy and the pack were still chanting: *Earth, air, fire, water!*

"Anya!" Mom was running towards me.

"Mom!"

She embraced me, and just as she did, the rain, the thunder, the wind, the shaking: all of it stopped. It went eerily silent. Mom and I stepped apart and all of us looked up at the sky. Even the animals below stopped their rampage and looked up.

We scanned around in all directions, but we saw nothing. The quiet loomed, and none of us said anything. We heard a click, and turned to see Robin, out of the car now, also scanning the sky.

Then I saw it. Stars winking on and off. The black shadow was on the horizon to the west. It seemed to be getting bigger.

"Its here!" Auntie Lily hissed, pointing her bony finger.

I looked harder. Where was it?

"Does anyone see it?" I whispered. No one answered. We just kept anxiously scanning the sky.

Then I heard it. A faint rustling. I started to say something, and then, so close I couldn't believe it, a *whoooooosh*, like the luffing of a huge sail, and as we turned to the noise, we saw that half of the stars in the sky were gone. The shadow moved directly over us, *whhooooo-OOOOOSH*, and began to circle the site. Then we heard another great rumbling below, as the animals began to abandon their rampage and run to safety. All the workers seemed long gone.

"This is it!" Mom cried. "Anya, the stone. Let me have it." Without hesitation, I handed Mom the stone. She held it in her hands and raised it high above her head, shouting to the sky:

Sha'thuun vekar Oma'shélun

No'kaar Dor'nai keluth

The stone instantly lit up with an intensely bright yellow light that shone straight up into the night. I stared at Mom, amazed. I had never heard her speak Tuhánee; I didn't even know she knew any. And here she stood, blasting powerful magic into the heavens. For a moment I lost sight of everything else. Then Mom turned to me, snapping me out of my daze.

"It's activated. The Watanuuk will come for it!" She warned.

"Everyone! Dance around the circle! Clockwise!" Auntie Lily bellowed. "Repeat the chant!"

The pack started dancing around the circle. Robin stood by, unsure what to do, until I gestured her in. "Dance!" I shouted at her. "Keep up the chant!"

Ethan entered the circle. Mom brought the stone down and looked at him. "Are you ready?"

Ethan nodded. He took my face in his hands. "I'll be right back." He kissed me quickly, and then stood back and breathed deep. In that breath, he was in eagle form. Mom extended the stone upward, and Ethan deftly snatched it in his talons.

As he did, I heard a terrifying howl from the sky, so shrill it hurt my ears, but at the same time so thunderous I could feel it in my spine. I could see Ethan getting smaller and smaller, the stone lighting him from below, until all I could see was the glow of the stone.

The Watanuuk was out there, but still, all we could see of him was a black shadow and the occasional glint of moonlight on his enormous wings. The yellow dot of the stone got smaller, coming nearer the black shadow, until the shadow darted, and Ethan dove suddenly, the stone swooping down towards the lights of the compound! The shadow darted after it, and for a second I could make out the dark shape of Ethan's wings, swooping through a tangle of pipes next to a large tank.

There, in the light, we almost could make out the form of the Watanuuk. But before we could register the horror of it, it dug an enormous talon into the tank, ripping it open, and there was a blinding flash, followed half a second later by a tremendous *WHUMP* that blew my hair back.

And that's when we saw It.

A spectacular ball of fire arose and curled around It as It hovered, It's great wings spinning the flames into whirlwinds. It's enormous body was covered in dark, mossy scales, Its wings shimmering with slick feathers of black and iridescent green. It's feet were webbed, but had gigantic black talons. Then It looked at us, It's head was shaped like a hawk's, but with a bizarre humanoid face and solid black eyes. It tucked it's claws upward from the flame and let out another terrifying howl, showing hideous pointed teeth.

The animals that had not managed to flee the compound already were scrambling madly as It flapped the flames downward at them, lit up in the hellish glow, a chunk of the tank still stuck on It's talon.

It's gaze stayed fixed on us, and we held our breath. It started to flap harder, gathering momentum in It's enormous bulk, heading in our direction. Then the orange star of the stone zipped by it's face, and the Watanuuk headed after it.

It took off after Ethan, gaining speed. We could see Ethan carving a wide arc around the site, and the Watanuuk followed. Ethan turned sharply towards the site and dove at top speed; in the lights of the compound we could see Ethan's wings almost touching the ground as it flew straight through the site, then we saw the bright stone rising into the night. But Ethan had flown too fast—by the time the Watanuuk reached the site, Ethan was far in the air, and the Watanuuk made a beeline for him, missing the site entirely.

Ethan made another wide, looping arc, moving slower now, and the Watanuuk again followed. But this time, Ethan, reaching the center of the site, and flew straight up. As the Watanuuk came up underneath him, Ethan put himself in a stall, falling in a spiral, coming within twenty feet on the Watanuuk's face, then tucking into a dive and zooming away.

I fought an urge to cover my eyes. "Just drop the stone on It already!!" I screamed. Mom touched my arm. "No," she said tersely, "he has to finish the job."

Ethan pulled up from the dive and swooped around, again coming dangerously close to the Watanuuk. Then he flew towards one of the cranes, headed straight for the top of the structure. He pulled up and climbed again, then stalled and spiraled again, as the Watanuuk drew nearer. He spiraled down, past the top of the crane, and just as he fell past the operator's cab, he tucked in his wings and dove into the shaft of the tower! We could see him, his dark shape and the bright stone, plunging through the scaffolding, down the center of the tower, as the Watanuuk headed straight for him.

I couldn't watch, and yet I couldn't look away. Inches above the bottom, Ethan soared out of the tower and zoomed along the ground.

Then the Watanuuk hit the crane.

The tower almost exploded from the impact, the heavy steel bars of the scaffolding scattering like matchsticks. The long horizontal arm of the crane, now supported by nothing, lurched sideways and fell heavily. The massive hook at the end of the arm was headed straight for another of the big tanks; the instant it made contact, there was another blinding flash, and, a half-second later, another deafening *WHUMP.*

Now the site was an inferno, the previous fire still raging, and a mushroom of fire rose high into the air from the new explosion. None of this seemed to affect the Watanuuk, except to further enrage it. It looked around, and seeing Ethan, flapped madly in his direction.

Ethan wheeled, heading straight for the Watanuuk's face. He pulled himself through the sky with great strokes of his wings, gathering speed. We all held our breath. This was it—he was going to release the stone.

But just as Ethan was going to let go, the Watanuuk flapped backwards, and with unbelievable speed, flicked one of his talons upwards, knocking Ethan wildly off course. We could see Ethan clutching the stone in his talon as he completely lost control. He spun through the air, turning over like a fighter plane with an engine on fire, the stone creating a bright spiral in the sky as he fell back to Earth. He crashed down on the ground. The stone, no longer in motion, was shining straight up in the air like a klieg light.

The pack all screamed, and before I could even think, I was shifted into my lion body and running top speed towards Ethan. Faye was in bear mode, and was running behind me.

I could hear Mom screaming from the top of the hill.

"Anya, no!!!"

Within seconds we were dashing through the compound, dodging flames and wreckage. I could see Ethan, still in his eagle form, in the distance. As I got closer, he stood, wobbling; I could see his wing was broken. He shifted into his human body, briefly glitching back and forth between his two forms, which somehow was much more upsetting than his injury. As we drew near, he finally shifted back to human, staggered weakly, and then collapsed hard onto the ground. The stone lay a few feet away, and I suddenly wanted to cry, thinking of the heroic effort it had taken for him to keep ahold of the stone.

Faye ran to Ethan, grabbing his collar and dragging him back towards the hill. Faye looked at me, and we both knew what I needed to do.

I grabbed the stone in my teeth and immediately started running. I saw the Watanuuk above, the firelight glistening off it's slick feathers and scales. It's eyes were locked on me, and it was terrifying. It was going to come after me until one of us was gone, and the only way at It was up. One of the cranes was still standing, and almost without thinking I knew it was my only hope. I sprinted full speed for the base of the tower.

The only way up was the ladder in the center of the scaffolding of the tower. The entryway was caged off by a heavy steel mesh door, but I merely jumped over the cage and leaped onto the scaffolding. My climbing abilities continued to amaze me as I was able to vault off the ladder and the scaffolding alternately, leaping up the tower unbelievably fast.

But the Watanuuk was faster. It looped around, and it looked like It wanted to gather speed, in order to better smash the crane to bits. I looked over my shoulder at the nauseating drop down the center of the tower. *Don't think about it.* I looked over and saw something moving on the ground, about fifty yards away. A trailer had been knocked on its side, and its front door was jerking and flapping up and down. Finally it flapped all the way open, and I saw Dan Gann prop his elbows on the doorframe and pull himself up.

He jumped off the side of the trailer and ran in the direction of the van, which stood untouched in the middle of all the chaos. I looked back toward the Watanuuk, dreading what I'd see. But It's eyes were on Dan, extremely conspicuous in his bright coat, running top speed across open ground.

He made it to the van; the keys must have been in it, because it started almost instantly. Still climbing frantically, I looked back at the Watanuuk, who now seemed entirely focused on Dan. I finally reached the operator's cab, just under the long horizontal arm of the crane, and I made frenzied calculations: *do I go out on the end of the arm? No, to the top of the tower. I need to be able to defend from all sides.* The tower extended another fifty feet or so above the arm, where huge cables suspended the arm in place.

As I climbed up around the cab, I saw Dan speeding away in the Sprinter Van. I turned to the Watanuuk just in time to see It— *WHOOOOOSH*—fly by the tower, blasting me with the wind off It's wings. I continued scrambling upwards as the Watanuuk swooped down and snatched the van off the ground, crumpling its sides, the accelerator gunning crazily as Dan tried to speed away in midair.

The Watanuuk flew upwards, the van dangling in its talons, and despite the fact Dan had left Robin and me for dead, the thought of him helpless in the van made me feel sick. Then the Watanuuk flicked It's great foot and flung the van off into the night, where it vanished into the dark, spinning, hundreds of feet in the air. *Don't think about it.*

I reached the top, where the crane's aircraft warning light swooped red beams through the sky. I shifted into human form, and braced myself in the scaffolding underneath the warning light, out of the way of its blinding beam. I felt so much smaller and more vulnerable hanging there, a frail human holding on for dear life. But I'd need my arms.

The Watanuuk swiveled It's head around. It's focus was back on me. I took a deep breath. It wheeled It's body in the sky and headed straight for me. I could sense its chaos, its pure destructive nature. It had no evil. It had no good. It simply was. It would destroy mindlessly until the balance was restored, and I was now in its sights. *All right then,* I thought, *here we go.*

The Watanuuk rushed straight forward, eyes locked on me and the stone. Closer, closer, until I could see the red light of the tower swooping across It's face. It opened It's mouth wide.

Closer, closer—*I'm not gonna put this stone on you, I'm going to put it IN you.* I looked at the back of its throat. *Whatever happens to me after, you are eating this thing.*

I threw the stone as hard as I could.

The flash and bang that happened—for a second I thought it was me dying. The Watanuuk's huge mass should have kept going straight through the crane, and straight through me. But bolts of lightning shot out from the creature, and it was flung backwards as though it had hit a giant wall. It hit the ground with a tremendous *THUMP*; the crane jarred so hard I lost my footing and fell. But my cat reflexes were quicker than my conscious mind, and I had grabbed onto a section of scaffold almost before I could realize it.

But instead of crumpling on the ground, the Watanuuk seemed to bounce off it, and now, instead of getting thrown backwards, It seemed to accelerate: It was getting *pulled* backwards, It's wings dragging in front of it, head down, as though an unseen force was dragging It by the back of the neck, into the air—hundreds of feet in the air—and It was swept away into the distance, in the direction of the lake, until I couldn't see It any more.

I hung there, swaying, for a moment. I swung my legs until I hooked them around a section of tower, and scooted in until I found my footing. I noticed that the sick feeling that had been building all these days had suddenly vanished. I hadn't realized how strong it was until it was gone.

No sooner had I felt this relief than another sickening anxiety took over—Ethan was hurt badly, and he needed my help. I could see Faye and the others gathered around him on the hill, and I shifted quickly. I had to get there fast.

My lion form found it quick work to jump down the tower; I took great leaps I couldn't imagine taking as a human. I sprung off at the base and hit the ground running, dashing across the compound and up the hill as fast as I could go.

Auntie Lily had her car running, and as I approached I instantly shifted back. Mom was in the back seat with Ethan. Robin and the rest of the pack were in Felix's car.

"We have to get him to Cave Rock. NOW!" Auntie Lily yelled. "Jimmy, get in the car with us!" Without questioning, Jimmy jumped out of Felix's car and got into the front seat with Auntie Lily. "Anya, get in with us. Felix, go get Ethan's dad and meet us at Cave Rock. GO NOW!"

"On it, Auntie Lily." Felix didn't hesitate, he just hit the pedal and went.

I jumped into the back seat with Mom, crying "Ethan! Ethan!" He didn't answer. His body was motionless laying across the back seat, his head in Mom's lap.

"He's not breathing!" Jimmy looked pale as he looked at Ethan.

Mom was holding him in her arms as tears fell down her cheeks. I lay across his chest, praying to hear a heartbeat. Nothing. Auntie Lily peeled out of the forest like a stunt driver.

"It's too long to drive," Mom argued, "maybe we should take him to the hospital."

"The hospital will put him in a bag. We're going to the lakefront and take the speedboat to Cave Rock. It's our only option," Lily yelled. With these words I cried harder, shaking Ethan's body.

"Our boat isn't working." I cried, panicking. Ethan's skin felt cold. "Don't you leave me," I cried, looking at his beautiful face, his lips a light blue. "You stay here." Hot tears were streaked down my face, my breath shaky and hollow.

"We're going to my boyfriend's house. He has a fast boat. He will take us." Auntie Lily said.

"Boyfriend!? You have a boyfriend?" Mom was shocked.

"I have several. But this one has the boat." Auntie Lily was driving the Mustang like a rally car, tearing off the dirt road and laying rubber onto the paved street, controlling the skid perfectly and snapping the car into a straight line. A fire truck whooshed by in the opposite direction, siren blaring, and we could see lights from the others in the distance.

Lily veered into the wrong lane, so far on the left I could hear rocks being thrown, then carved a right turn onto a side road, coming within inches of a telephone pole. Ahead, I saw one of those large, fancy stucco mailboxes. As we approached, She whipped the car left, past it, and dove down a wide driveway. At the end of it was a palatial lakefront home.

Jimmy squinted, confused. "*This* is your boyfriend's house?" Auntie Lily squealed to a stop and laid on the horn.

A man came running out the front door. He looked much younger than Lily and was dressed in a red velvet robe. She got out and ran to him; I could see her gesturing to him wildly. He pointed to the dock and ran back inside the house.

Auntie Lily hustled over to the car.

"He's putting on pants and meeting us at the dock. We have to get Ethan to the boat, right now!" Auntie Lily ran to the dock.

Mom jumped out of the car and we all lifted Ethan together. He was so heavy; we struggled with him as we hurried down the path to the dock.

Auntie's boyfriend was running up to us, fully dressed.

"I'm Marco. Here let me carry him." Marco took Ethan from us, his face filled with concern after seeing Ethan's color.

Marco ran faster down the dock and to the boat. Lily was ahead, and had already reached the speedboat, its engine deeply burbling. "Unmoor us!" Lily yelled. Mom began unwrapping the lines from the cleats on the dock and throwing them into the boat.

"Anya, I'm going to save him." Jimmy had tears in his eyes. "I don't know how, but I come from a long line of shamans. The Eshooni will breathe life into Ethan. I'll make them."

We climbed into the boat. Marco laid Ethan across the rear seats and sat next to him, holding him steady.

"They won't kill you, Jimmy. You're the shaman. You will be welcomed. But we cannot go in," Lily said, slamming the throttle and tearing away from the dock.

Dawn was coming on; a dim glow illuminated everything. I stared out onto the water, the cold wind whipping my hair into my face, strands of hair stuck to the tear trails on my cheeks. I was breathing and crying the way a toddler does, huffing spasmodically. Mom steadied herself and sat on the floor on the boat, hugging onto my legs.

"We're going to do everything we can." Mom was crying too.

"Are you sure we shouldn't we take him to a hospital?" I gurgled.

"It's too late for hospitals," Lily yelled from the driver's seat. "He needs something more."

The boat jumped and skipped over the choppy waters and slammed up and down on the lake as Lily held onto the wheel with white knuckles, her eyes fixed on Cave Rock.

"What do I do? How do I do this?" Jimmy looked at Mom, terrified.

"We're taking him to the Lady of the Lake. You bring him inside the cave," Mom yelled, over the roar of the engine. "Put him in the water inside the cave. Summon the Eshooni, thank them, and ask for their guidance. Tell them Ethan needs his life back. They have been known to bring back the dead. It's happened before." Mom squeezed Jimmy's hand. "You are so powerful, Jimmy. Listen to your inner voice. You will be guided."

I stared at Ethan's body and wondered where he was. I couldn't hear him, couldn't feel his presence. Was he in the library with Frederick? Was he inside his body, waiting for us to save him? Was he flying as an eagle someplace? Was he completely dead and in some other dimension? Ethan was not here. He was not in this boat with us and I wanted to know where the hell he was!

"Where is he?" I cried, looking at him. "Where is Ethan?"

"Anya. I'm going into that cave and I'm going to go get him, OK? I'm going to get him back and put him back in his body." Jimmy was confident and stern, his tears drying up as his purpose was clear.

I could see Cave Rock ahead. It was majestic, looming hundreds of feet above the lake.

Auntie Lily slowed the boat down as we approached the shoreline. "Here we are," she hollered, "the Lady of the Lake." Up to this point, I hadn't been sure whether we were going to see an actual lady. But now I looked up at the rock, and saw, jutting out over the lake, a rock formation that looked exactly like a woman's profile, silhouetted perfectly against the glow of the coming dawn. Lily put the boat directly under the Lady, then wheeled it around and put it in reverse, gently pushing the stern as close as possible to the cliff. Lily cut the engines, and we heard a little splash as she released the anchor.

I looked up at the forbidding overhang, and turned to Lily. "How are we getting him up there?"

"We aren't going up. We go down." Lily pointed to the water.

Marco folded down the swim ladder over the stern. "The rest of you stay in the boat. I have to go in alone." Jimmy said.

"I won't leave Ethan. I have to go in," I stated flatly.

"The cave won't admit women," Lily said. "It's just the way it is."

I shifted into my lion form, and jumped in the water.

"Anya!" Mom yelled. "You can't go into the cave!"

"Well, technically, she can go in now." Auntie Lily said, "the ancestors said women. They didn't say anything about female lions." She shrugged. "Either way, she can try. The cave will admit her or it won't."

I swam around to the ladder. Jimmy and Marco were struggling to get Ethan in the water without being too rough.

"Here," Jimmy said, "put him on Anya's back. Here." Jimmy entered the water. "Oh my God! Cold cold cold! Ahhhh!" He steadied himself on a rock and stood about waist-deep. "Sorry. It's just really cold. Here." He took Ethan into the water and gestured for me to sink down. I did, and he draped Ethan across my neck. He sunk down to chin-deep. "Ohh! So cold! Whoo." He brought one of Ethan's arms and one of his legs to my mouth. "OK Anya, bite down on his sleeve and his pant leg and hold on tight. We're going under."

Jimmy took a deep breath, preparing to dive. "Hey, wait." He stopped and looked up at the boat. "What am I looking for?!"

"The rock will show you," Lily said calmly.

He took another deep breath and we plunged under. Dawn was coming on outside, but underwater it was still very dark. Even my cat vision strained to see anything but a blur of large, mossy boulders going almost straight down. I looked at Jimmy, and we swam deeper.

Further down, I saw an area where the rocks were bare, the only ones not sporting a thick fur of moss. I swam down for a closer look. The largest rock seemed to have a dark squiggle on it, and I looked up, trying to get Jimmy's attention. I was in deeper than I thought. But Jimmy saw me, and with some effort he managed to get to me.

As he drew closer, the dark squiggle became luminescent, glowing a faint blue. It revealed a pattern of concentric circles, flanked on either side by two humanoid figures with gigantic round heads. The nearer Jimmy went, the brighter they glowed. He reached out and touched the circle with his hand.

As he did there was a trembling, and the rock above it fell to the side, coming to rest on another boulder. There was a hole behind, just large enough to swim through. Jimmy started to swim towards it, but it seemed to suck him in, and he vanished.

Alarmed, I swam over and found myself suddenly sucked into the passage. I bit down hard on Ethan's clothes, and tucked my legs in as close as I could, tumbling in the darkness until I found myself spat out, my head out of the water. I gasped for breath, and I could hear Jimmy breathing hard. It was utterly pitch black; even with my cat eyes I couldn't see anything. I started to panic—in our hurry to help Ethan, we hadn't even considered how to light the cave. Should I leave Ethan with Jimmy and swim back out for some kind of light? How would I even find the hole? Would our flashlights work under-water? Did we even have any?

The water inside the cave was weirdly warm. I felt around with my paws and felt a shallow incline. I fumbled my way up it and realized I was coming out of the water; I huffed a little, hoping Jimmy would understand to follow me, and laid Ethan down on dry ground. I could hear Jimmy splashing up the incline, and then felt him next to me. We were OK. Now what?

Just then, the water started to glow. Very dimly at first, but now I could see we were in a large cave, and the three of us were on a smooth rock formation that sloped gently into the water, like a little beach. The water glowed brighter, a blue light that shimmered up on the walls of the caves, which were covered in beautiful petroglyphs. They were obviously ancient, but unlike the pictures of Native petro-glyphs I'd seen, they weren't worn or faded. They could have been made yesterday. Jimmy and I looked around in awe. And then the Eshooni arrived.

I saw the passage to the lake light up, and three glowing lights entered. They were about the size and shape of koi fish, but made, it seemed, only of light. The lights stopped in the pool of warm water, and held there, still. Jimmy and I stood.

I felt overwhelmed with a need to be with Ethan in my human form, and felt a rising panic again. Would I harm the magic? Would I be thrust from the cave? Would Ethan be left to die? I looked at the Eshooni and felt a sudden calm. My feelings were in tune. I could feel a harmony. I took a deep breath, closed my eyes, and shifted.

I opened my eyes. Nothing had happened. The Eshooni floated placidly. I looked over at Jimmy, and he looked at me. We gently took Ethan and placed him in the water, his head resting on the rock.

Jimmy faced the water. He held his head high and spoke in a strong, clear voice. "I am Jimmy Duncan, from the ancestors of the Pine Nut Mountains. I have been called by the dreams. My friend, my brother, Ethan, lost his life protecting his people from the forces of chaos and restoring the balance of our beautiful world. I humbly ask that you restore him from the spirit world, so he can be with his people a while longer."

Jimmy stood proudly. The Eshooni floated, still. I suddenly felt an overwhelming sense of calm and peace, the panic and confusion of the past days simply washing away. I could feel that Jimmy felt it, too. He began singing a low, ancient, wordless tune.

The Eshooni moved forward, up the shore on either side of Ethan, and—I guess stood is the word—stood out of the water, glowing in the shape of a droplet, about two feet tall, but simply made of light. As they approached, Jimmy and I moved back. One stood above Ethan's head, the other two at each shoulder. Then they seemed to melt into a puddle that surrounded Ethan. I saw the upsetting kink in his broken arm straighten as the Eshooni surrounded him, covering him in a bluish light.

Then they swam off into the water, and floated there. I stood there for some time, having no idea what came next, but still utterly calm. Then Ethan breathed.

Jimmy and I fell on him, sobbing with joy. He began to stir, and his eyes opened. I embraced him, my tears smearing on his face. Jimmy and I sat him up, looking into his eyes, sobbing and grinning like idiots.

He gave his head a little shake. "Whoa."

Jimmy and I burst into laughter, giggling and crying at the same time.

Ethan looked around. "So, we're in a cave…"

We laughed even harder, fighting to speak.

After a bit I managed to blurt out, "Look!" I pointed to the water, "the Eshooni!"

Ethan looked at them in amazement. "So, how dead was I?"

We cracked up all over again. "Sufficiently," I said.

"Dude…" Jimmy managed to speak. "You were extremely dead."

"You still looked good, though," I sputtered. "Blue looks good on you." We laughed until we were done, then, wiping the tears from our eyes, we helped Ethan to his feet.

"How do you feel?" Jimmy asked.

"It's weird; I feel great, actually," Ethan replied, "better than before."

The Eshooni began to circle the passage in the clear pond. "All right, we'd better get back. It's a lot colder on the other side, but the boat is right there. Are you ready?"

We looked at one another, smiled, and then Jimmy dove in, Ethan and I after. We saw the Eshooni zip through the tunnel, and we were whooshed through the passageway into the icy lake.

We came to the surface to a brilliant sunrise, and immediately heard cheering from the boat. We scrambled up the ladder, Mom and Lily and Marco taking turns hugging us all, tears of joy streaming down their faces. We heard a *screeech* from the shore, and turned to see Luke and Felix's cars pulling up on the shore road. Felix, Lucy, Faye, Terra, Iris, Robin and Luke piled out, yelling and jumping and waving their arms, overjoyed. We jumped and waved back.

Auntie Lily lit a cigarillo. "I don't know about you, but I'm starving. Is it too early for pizza?"

<hr>

Two days after the Watanuuk was put in it's nest Robin was going back to Los Angeles.

The pack of us—me, Ethan, Jimmy, Felix, Iris, Lucy, Faye, and Robin—clambered up the steps to my house and stacked our snowboards on the porch. As we stomped the snow from our boots I opened the front door, releasing an intoxicating aroma of lasagna and woodsmoke.

"Oh man," cried Ethan, "that smells amazing! I'm starving!"

We had started pulling off our jackets and snow pants when Robin suddenly ran toward the kitchen door, her jacket and pants still on, and grabbed her dad, Jay, who had just emerged from the kitchen, in a huge hug. They embraced a long time.

"Man, am I glad to see you, kid," he said to Robin, holding her face in his hands. He looked up and saw me. "And you too, Anya!" I ran to him and hugged both of them.

Mom, Auntie Lily, and Luke came in from the kitchen. "Good run today?" Mom asked. "Excellent!" I said.

"So, are you ready to move here yet?" Auntie Lily asked Robin. "It's definitely not boring." Robin laughed.

"This sure isn't an easy place to get to! Your storms are insane." Jay chuckled.

"We shouldn't have any more freak storms," Auntie Lily said, smiling.

Out of the corner of my eye, I saw Fancy Beast trotting down the stairs, carrying something large and black in her mouth. She wove her way through all the people, walked up to me, and dropped the stuffed Watanuuk at my feet.

I clapped my hands to my mouth. "Oh my God!" I said, laughing. "Robin, I completely forgot. I got you a present. My first day in Emerald." I grabbed the Watanuuk and held it out to her, and everyone practically fell over laughing.

Everyone except Jay, of course. "What's the joke? I don't get it."

"Just some ancient Tuhánee legend. It's a long story," Mom said, wiping tears from her eyes.

Robin ran over and took it from me. "I will cherish this forever. It's the best souvenir I've ever had!" Robin grabbed onto me and hugged tightly.

That night I lay in bed, feeling the good aches from a long day of snowboarding. The pine candle was lit and it filled the room with a warm, woodsy scent. Fancy Beast was squashed up next to me, snoozing happily. I smiled, looking around my room and feeling less lost than I had in a long time. I looked out the window at the gentle snowfall. An eagle swooped down and landed on the deck railing.

ABOUT THE AUTHOR

Beth Colla is an author, artist, and proud mom living in Hollywood, California. A graduate of the legendary Second City, she weaves humor, heart, and a dash of mischief into everything she creates. Her debut novel—first in a spellbinding series—ventures deep into the supernatural world of therians, a concept inspired by her daughter, Daisy, whose curiosity and adventurous spirit sparked the story's beating heart.

When she's not dreaming up tales of magic, transformation, and friendship, Beth can be found painting, tinkering with creative projects, or doting on her Pomeranian sidekick, Finneas. (Both Beth and Finn firmly believe cheese and naps are essential to the creative process.)

This book marks the start of a wild and wonderful journey into a world where magic is real and friendship changes everything.

instagram.com/wakingthewild
tiktok.com/@wakingthewild